DATE DUE

Martin Shannon

A NOVEL BY

ROBERT BUCKLEY

Cover by Michael J. Buckley

Text set in Georgia

Manufactured in the United States of America

3 5 7 9 10 8 6 4

Library of Congress Control Number

ISBN: 978-1727020250

Other works by Robert Buckley

The Slave Tag

Ophelia's Brooch

Two Miles An Hour

The Denarius

I'm Lost Again

1

SCARTAGLEN, COUNTY KERRY,
IRELAND

1860

Sixteen-year-old Martin Shannon was large for his age. A strapping young man with deep blue eyes and a mop of dark brown hair. He'd spent most of his young life outside in the fresh salty air and his ruddy complexion proved it.

At the moment, he was carefully and quietly working his way through a thick patch of gorse that was clinging to the edge of a cliff.

Off in the distance the flinty grey waters of the churning North Atlantic glinted up at him.

He was looking down at a rabbit warren that was well-hidden at the base of a large and ancient larch tree. The tree was tilted at an unnatural angle, the result of centuries of serious winds that blew down from the County Kerry hills.

The rabbit warren had been a constant source of food for Martin's family ever since he'd accidentally found it the past spring.

He was on his way to check the snare he'd set at dusk the evening before. But he had to be careful. He was trespassing on private land and surely didn't want to be caught again by Patrick McGuinness, Lord Gilroy's gamekeeper.

Sure enough, sometime during the night another hapless rabbit had shuffled down the narrow trail, squeezed between the rocks and slipped its neck into the snare before it realized what was happening.

The branch snapped up and after a minute of frantic struggling, it was all over. Martin couldn't believe rabbits were that dumb but he wasn't about to complain.

He quickly crept down the trail and slipped the rabbit out of the noose, reset the snare and snuck quietly away. It was a nice, plump one and the second of the morning. His ma would be pleased – as long as she didn't find out he was poaching again.

Martin got caught poaching a year earlier. He was tickling fish out of one of Lord Gilroy's private trout streams. It wasn't the first time he'd taken Lord Gilroy's trout – but it was the first time he'd been caught.

He'd been taught the art of tickling by a master; old Ciaran Joyce.

"Stealth," whispered Ciaran early one morning as they quietly snuck together out of the woods. "Stealth and a steady hand."

Martin watched as the old rebel crept up to the edge of the stream and slowly slipped his bony arm into a deep pool, inch by inch.

"Can't spook 'em laddie," he softly murmured. "Just be gentle and reach down 'n tickle 'em under the belly 'til they relax and then ..."

At this point the old man reared back and flipped a beautiful big trout onto the bank and cackled, "... tickle it out and into the frypan."

Martin knew what he was doing was forbidden as well as dangerous, but as old Ciaran pointed out, there were several streams running through the master's property, and they were all thick with trout. "God put 'em there for a purpose, laddie. It'd surely be a sin to waste 'em."

It was early dusk when he'd been caught.

A small herd of handsome Red deer were just coming out of the woods to feed in the lush meadow.

In deep concentration Martin began working his way to the stream – slowly and surely. It never occurred to him that McGuinness might be watching this particular meadow with a glass, checking the size and number of the beautiful animals that roamed his master's vast property.

But unfortunately for Martin, that's exactly what he was doing and he easily spotted the boy creeping up to the edge of the water.

Surprised at what he saw, McGuinness sat quietly on his bog pony and watched.

Martin choose a quiet pool where a partially sunken log was close to the bank. He knelt softly and slipped his hand down into the water, past his elbow, while McGuinness watched him intently.

"The hell's he doing?" McGuinness whispered to himself. Then it dawned on him. "By God, he's tickling fish! Look at him .... that little shite's done this before."

At that very moment, Martin reared back, flipping a fish onto the bank behind him. It was a beauty. A large, fat German Brown, at least four pounds, a wonderful surprise for his mother's 48th birthday and enough to feed the entire family.

He yanked a handful of watercress out of the cold, swift running water and stuffed it in a sack along with the trout and rushed away with his prize.

He'd gone about a half mile when he saw McGuinness cantering across the field toward him cutting him off from his path home.

With his heart in his mouth, Martin stopped running and watched as the gamekeeper trotted up, dismounted and walked up to him.

He knew Patrick McGuinness from afar. A large, man. Tanned and lined from a life outdoors in all kinds of weather.

"Fair, but strict," most people said about him. But he was an Irishman who worked for an Englishman and that outweighed any positive feelings the locals may have had for him. He usually drank alone in the pub.

"What's in yer bag, young Martin?" McGuinness asked as he walked up to him, effectively blocking any hope of running off, even though it would have been a useless and humiliating endeavor. McGuinness knew where he lived.

"Just a few turnips," stammered Martin, sounding guilty as sin. His eyes looked everywhere except at McGuinness' face.

"Turnips, is it?" said McGuinness staring at the bag Martin was holding close by his side, willing it to disappear.

"*Wet* turnips, by the looks of it."

Martin looked down. Indeed, water was dripping down onto his leg. If he only hadn't stuffed in so much watercress. He didn't look back up. He was caught red-handed. He knew what would happen next.

"Gimme the bag, laddie," McGuinness said. "Let's have a look at those wet turnips."

Martin dejectedly handed him the bag and McGuinness peered in.

"What be ye thinking, Martin? Are ye daft, laddie? That's yer landlord's stream you're poaching."

"Sorry," whimpered Martin. "It's my ma's birthday. No money to buy her nothing. Won't do it again. I promise."

"Maybe ye won't. Maybe ye will. Looks to me like you've had plenty of practice. I seen you tickle that trout out. Turn 'round and drop your britches!"

Martin did as he was told and tried to steel himself for the first blow.

McGuinness took his crop and gave him five sharp cracks on his exposed buttocks, not hard enough to break the skin but hard enough to leave livid welts he'd have for a few days. The swift punishment was over in less than a minute.

Martin didn't cry out, but tears streamed down his face. It was his pride that was really hurting.

"Now, turn around and get home. And run! I'll be right behind ye. I wanna talk to yer da about this."

2

John and Cathleen Shannon were already standing in front of their tiny cottage when Martin, closely followed by Patrick McGuinness, came up the lane.

They'd been alerted by their seven-year-old daughter, Colleen, and they were all standing in the fading light, sensing something unfortunate had happened. Martin stumbled to a halt in front of his parents, wiping his eyes dry with his shirt sleeve.

McGuinness had known Cathleen Shannon since they were barefoot school kids together – before the new laws had passed. He'd always been sweet on her but shortly after his twentieth birthday he'd left for Dublin to fuel a young man's fire of adventure.

Two years passed before he quietly returned to the village, fed up with the hectic city life and much subdued. Perhaps ready to marry and settle down.

If he had Cathleen on his mind, it was too late. She was already married and had a child.

Truth be known she was already with child before she married. She swore she'd been taken down by gypsies one night coming back from picking berries. She was too ashamed to tell anyone the truth and by the time she showed, it was way too late.

Most people took her at her word. But the tongue waggers couldn't help but notice that the sorry episode coincided neatly with Patrick McGuinness' departure for Dublin.

Nevertheless, John Shannon was man enough to take her into marriage and overlook any foolish gossip. And that pretty much put an end to any more talk about it. That and an event that took place one night in O'Donahue's Pub when an ugly soul, mouthy on whiskey, made a disparaging remark about Cathleen Shannon being a pushover for 'gypsies.'

Patrick McGuinness overheard him and without a moment's hesitation – and with one mighty blow – flattened his nose and knocked out two front teeth. And that *was* the end of it.

"John ... Cathleen," said McGuinness as he trotted up and came to a stop in front the cottage. The smoke of their peat fire swirled lazily in the air.

"Patrick," said Cathleen in a soft voice searching her son's face for clues.

Martin's father nodded silently, staring up at the man on the horse. He knew him, of course, and had heard the stories about him and his wife.

"Caught the lad poaching, John," said McGuinness.

John's eyes snapped to his son and his mouth dropped open in surprise.

"Took a trophy salmon out of himself's private stream. Had to cane him."

Startled at this additional piece of news his father went over to the boy and pulled his trousers down far enough to show the puffy stripes. He winced.

"Good God, man," he said, staring with malevolence at the gamekeeper. "He's just a boy."

"He's old enough to catch trout by hand and he's old enough to know better," said McGuinness in a loud voice, not backing down. "And I doubt it was the first time."

"He's just a boy," said John again, with less steam.

"You're right, John. He's just a boy," said McGuinness. "If he was a man, he coulda been hanged. It's happened other places. Ain't my rules. And you all know the rules. I'm paid to enforce 'em and I need this job. I've gotta family of my own that needs tending."

For a moment there was just silence. John Shannon looked like he'd been beaten himself as the grave injustice of it all swept over him like a foul cloud.

9

Cathleen Shannon just lowered her head and pulled her daughter, Colleen, into her bosom and rocked silently back and forth.

McGuinness looked down at Martin and said, "Remember yer promise, Martin? It'll not happen again? What?"

Martin didn't look up but nodded his head and said, "No, sir."

"Right then," said the gamekeeper as he turned and trotted his horse back down the lane, looking the other way as he let the sack with the trophy salmon slip to the ground.

3

By 1860 the potato famine had 'officially' ended in Ireland. But the scars it left on the hearts and souls of the Irish people were slow to heal. Widespread starvation had passed, but the Irish sense of family would never be the same.

For years, those who could manage it had been shipping their children to America. They no longer had any future living in Ireland and working as serfs for English landlords. Better off they'd be in America where friends and relatives were happy to have them and often helped with the passage money.

Now Ireland was about to lose three more.

A small crowd of friends and neighbors came to Moira and Sean Brogan's cabin for the going away party. No one was invited, but word spread and, after all, a party was a party.

In the desperate times being what they were, anything even resembling a party was a welcome relief. To call it a *party*, however, would surely be a misuse of the word. In reality, it was more like a wake and indeed the Brogans felt like they were dying inside. Their 21-year-old son, Brennan, and their 15-year old daughter, Mary, were leaving for America in the morning.

Going along with them was Martin Shannon, only son of their closest friends across the glen.

Everyone knew they would never see the children again. But no one would dare voice the words.

Moira Brogan and Cathleen Shannon were in the tiny kitchen cooking up a large kettle of stew using the two rabbits Martin had turned up with the day before. Blended together with a handful of onions, carrots and green beans along with a few scraps of fatback which John had traded a half day's labor for – it would be tasty enough.

Bridget and John Shaheen arrived with their five children and a wicker basket of rock-hard biscuits; Johanna and Timothy Buckley brought a pot of boiled potatoes; and others brought what they could spare. If it wasn't food, it was a few coins for the trip.

A fiddler and a penny whistler from O'Donahue's came to liven things up for the promise of a warm meal. And Paddy O'Brien, God bless his wicked soul, had managed to stagger in with a mostly-full jug of poteen.

The men, smiling in anticipation of sharing a jar, were already gathering in the parlor of the tiny cottage.

The night went well enough. There was plenty of food to eat and sufficient poteen to loosen up singing voices. Youngsters ran wild and played games. The teenagers and older kids huddled together and talked about the morning departure.

Inside, maudlin toasts were kept to a minimum and brave faces were worn by all.

Then, at deep dusk, came the surprise of the evening. A barking dog alerted the crowd and Sean Brogan went out to see who was arriving so late. It was Patrick McGuinness trotting up on his bog pony.

"Evening, Sean," said McGuinness from the saddle. "Hope the party's going well."

"Going well enough, Patrick," said Sean through tight jaws. "You're welcome to come in for a drop."

"No, thank you kindly," said McGuinness. "Just stopped by with something for the young folks to take with 'em. Heard they're leaving in the morning and thought this might come in handy."

He leaned down and dropped a large package in Brogan's hands.

"Venison. Jerked it myself. Should last 'em awhile if they pace it out."

Brogan stared at the package like it was solid gold and looked back up. "Mighty decent of you, Patrick. I know they'll appreciate it."

"And Lord Gilroy asked me to bring this over for 'em as well."

He bent down again and dropped three shilling coins in his hand. "Best sew 'em away for an emergency."

Sean stared at them in amazement. "Well, I don't know what to say, Patrick. These will be a huge help, for sure. Please take our thanks to himself."

"I will, of course," said Patrick. "He's a fair man, he is, when you give him a chance. And tell 'em good luck for me as well," he said as he turned to leave.

"We'll do that, Patrick. Many thanks again.

"Holy Mother," he muttered to himself as the pony trotted off, "I haven't seen a shilling in over a year."

By 8:00 p.m. people were beginning to return to their homes. The two families needed time to get the young adults ready to leave at first light.

It would be a three-day trip to reach the port of Cork and last minute details needed to be tended to. Little rest would be realized that night.

Martin had a shoulder pack and a small, cloth carry bag. Brennan and Mary each had packs, although Brennan's was larger and heavier. Two changes of clothes apiece, a light jacket, extra socks and a few personal items. The venison was divided up with instructions to be used sparingly.

The two young men carried sturdy walking sticks to ward off any dogs or unwelcome behavior from strangers. Poverty was still everywhere and people were desperate. Brennan and Martin could take care of themselves, but the Brogans were fearful for Mary.

Moira sewed the three shilling coins in the hem of Brennan's jacket with a warning to keep them out of sight, and to be used only in a dire emergency.

4

They left at daybreak, laden with promises to write faithfully and return home to visit in a year or two.

Moira Brogan was so devastated she could hardly get out of bed to see them off. Sean Brogan put on a calm face but on the inside was ready to collapse.

Martin had walked over alone, having earlier said his sad goodbyes to his own family.

"It's a day's walk to Boherbue Cross," said Mr. Brogan. "Spend a few pennies for a space at Sheedy's – and get some rest. One more day to Mallow. Your Aunt Deirdre's expecting you before dark. They'll cart you to Cork from there.

"Once you get to the docks, you have the agent's name and address. The papers say the boat leaves at high tide Wednesday evening ... weather permitting. If it's delayed, he'll arrange a place to stay and feed you. It's part of the fare, so don't let him charge you a farthing more."

They set off at a fast clip, Brennan and Martin in great spirits for the grand adventure of it all. Mary crying softly to herself and threatening to turn back until Brennan told her there was no turning back. It would just make matters worse and harder on ma.

They kept going, reaching Sheedy's Inn at twilight.

To call it an "inn" would take a definite stretch of the imagination. At best it was an earthy, dirt floor pub, with an attached shed where one could shelter and feed a horse and a space to spread out some straw and rest for the night. Sheedy was known as a hard man and left the missus to handle the travelers.

As tired as the three of them were, it was still a restless night at best. The rowdiness from the pub, the shifting of the horses rubbing against the sides of the shed, the barking dogs and the unfamiliarity of it all took its toll. That and the cold morning realization that there was, in fact, no turning back at this point.

Accommodations included use of a pump to wash up with, a cup of weak tea and a boiled potato in the morning.

Mrs. Sheedy took pity on the three of them and snuck them a thick hunk of soda bread from under her apron, making sure himself didn't see.

A heavy mist hung over the fields and enveloped them in its clammy arms as they left the shed and continued east. To add insult to injury, half way though their 12-mile walk, a light yet persistent rain blew in from the sea forcing them to stop and warm up under one of the many pack bridges they passed. A small fire, a sip of branch water and a sliver of venison to chew on and they were soon ready to keep going.

"How much farther, Brennan?" asked Mary, at this point wet and miserable.

"D'know," said Brennan. "Can't be more than a few miles, maybe three or four is all. Gotta keep moving, be getting dark soon."

"Let me carry your pack awhile, Mary," said Martin. "Best cover your head. You'll catch cold."

"Nah," said Mary straightening her shoulders and putting on a brave face. "I'm fine. Thanks anyhow."

Deirdre Quinn had been sitting by the window in her small parlor for the past two hours, her eyes glued to the road, watching for her niece and nephew to magically appear. It was way past dusk and they were long overdue.

When her younger sister, Moira, had asked if she would take them and Martin in for the night, she had happily agreed but now she was getting frantic. They couldn't have gotten lost, could they? Were they set upon by gypsies? Did they even leave home yesterday as planned?

She was about to send her husband, Francis, out with the cart when suddenly she spied them trudging up the road looking soaked and bedraggled.

"Saints Be Blessed," she muttered in relief as she jumped up and ran to put on the kettle.

"What kept you children?" she asked as they filed into the cottage. "I was terribly worried something happened to you."

"We're sorry, Aunt Deirdre," said Mary. "We left Sheedy's later than planned, and the rain slowed us down."

"We stopped to build a fire and dry out a little," said Brennan, "and we might have made a wrong turn a few miles back."

"Well never mind now," Aunt Deirdre said. "You're here safe enough, Praise the Lord. And this must be Martin Shannon."

"Yes, ma'am," said Martin. "My ma sends her greetings."

"Well I'm glad to hear it. I've known her since she was about this one's age," she said, giving Mary a big hug.

"Oh my goodness," she yelped, jumping back. "You're soaking wet, child! Let's get you all into some dry clothes before you catch your deaths.

"Mary, you'll stay with me tonight in the back room and the boys and himself will spread out in the parlor. There's plenty of room and it's warm and dry. He'll be here in a minute. He's putting the animals away. So get out of those wet clothes and I'll hang them by the fire to dry out. Then I'll fix us all something to eat. You must be famished."

Cups of hot tea, steaming bowls of vegetable soup, thick slabs of warm soda bread slathered with butter and a surprise sweet for each of them that Uncle Francis pulled out of his pocket. What a wonderful meal.

"Now before you all fall asleep at the table," said Aunt Deirdre, "let's go into the parlor and hear about this grand adventure you're having. You need to get to bed soon but I've a few questions to ask first. We're leaving in the cart at first light. I want to get you to the docks early in the afternoon. Moira said your ship leaves on the evening tide tomorrow, is that right?"

"Yes, ma'am," said Brennan, "the agent told us they usually leave around 5:00 or 6:00 p.m. But if they have to wait another day or two, he has to find us a place to stay and feed us. It's in the contract."

He patted his pocket for emphasis.

"Well then," said Aunt Deirdre, "that's fine for sure. Tis a long trip?"

"We're taking one of the newer steamers," said Brennan. "Trip's only two weeks or so. Maybe less. Much faster than the sailing ships."

"Well that's lovely. And your cousin Michael is meeting you in New York when you arrive, right?"

"No, ma'am. He's meeting us in Chicago," said Brennan. "Martin's staying in New York but Mary and I are going on by train to Chicago by ourselves.

It's all written out and we've got money for the tickets. Just one night on the train."

"And *then* you'll continue to Iowa to stay with your brother, James," said Aunt Deirdre. "Well, now, ain't I proud of you all, indeed. And you, Mary, aren't you a wee bit scared?"

"No, Auntie," said Mary in a soft voice as she began to tear up, "but I miss ma."

"Oh, I know you do, lamb," said Aunt Deirdre drawing Mary to her for a hug. "Don't cry, dear. You'll be fine. I know you all will. It's for the best. But it's getting late and we all need some sleep.

"Mary, you come with me. You men find a place to spread out and get some rest."

5

The rain blew off during the night and the promise of a lovely day began at sunrise.

Groggy and stiff after a heavy night's sleep, the boys joined Mary and Aunt Deirdre in the kitchen for cups of hot tea and sugar-coated scones.

Uncle Francis had already gone out and hitched up the cart. He tossed a few dusty blankets in the back for the youngsters to sit on and wrap up with against the chill.

Jenny, the aging pony, stood by obediently, stomping her hoof in anticipation of the trip ahead.

They arrived at Cork at half ten. The dock area was easy to find but the hustle and bustle was alarming. Dozens of large boats were tied up at several different piers and thousands of passengers were milling about in bewilderment.

They stopped and asked several people before they were able to find the correct shipping office where they went in and presented their papers.

"Well, we won't be ready to leave this evening," said the stressed agent. "We're a bit behind schedule loading supplies and such, but don't you worry none. You can stay on board tonight. We'll leave at high tide early in the morning, for sure.

"Your boat's just across the way," he said pointing to a large iron steamship with the name *Golden Dawn* painted in large white letters on the bow. A heavy wooden boarding plank led up to the main deck. It was already crowded with passengers and workmen going both ways.

"Shall they be getting on now?" asked Aunt Deirdre with spreading concern on her face.

"They can indeed," said the agent. "But won't be any meals served tonight. Best to get something to eat now. Plenty of time to come back and get settled later."

"Right then," said Uncle Francis. "We passed a small inn a short ways back. We'll all have a nice meal together before you board and your aunt and I head back to do chores."

The *Lantern* was crowded when they arrived. Francis tied Jenny up to a post and found a place where they could keep an eye on things. It was only midafternoon but it appeared that the stout had been flowing freely for most of the day.

A mixed bunch of sailors, dock laborers, ruffians and bewildered, immigrating family members crowded around what tables that were available.

They ended up sitting outside on the ground where they shared a large bowl of greasy mutton stew and a loaf of stale bread. Not exactly what Aunt Deirdre had hoped for in a proper farewell meal, but it would have to do.

Within an hour they were back at the *Golden Dawn* where the activity was even more intense than earlier.

After handshakes and hugs and a parcel of hard cheese passed to Brennan for the trip, the three of them showed their papers and headed up the plank.

Aunt Deirdre and Uncle Francis watched to make sure they got up on the main deck before turning the cart around and heading for home. Aunt Deirdre was waving frantically as they left.

The three of them were now officially on their own.

Reaching the main deck, they again showed their papers to a steward and led to a steep and narrow stairway labeled *Steerage C,* one of four steerage areas on the boat.

"This is *your* place, *Steerage C,*" he said taking down their names. "You'll find room to stay down below. It'll be yours for the voyage. Can't move around. Best get down now and find a proper place."

The three of them went down the stairs and entered a large room already half filled with people jostling to stake out their living spaces for the long voyage to New York.

The room was divided lengthwise by two aisles. Along both sides of the two aisles were 50 spaces, 25 on a side facing each other; 100 spaces in all.

The spaces, almost like cattle stalls, were separated from each other by five-foot, wood plank walls. Each space was considered enough room for four people, adults or children, no difference.

Dimly lit, the room already reeked of unwashed bodies.

"We should have come down earlier," said Martin looking around in a panic. "Almost every place looks taken."

"Over in the corner," Brennan shouted, rushing to the right. "C'mon, let's grab it before anyone else does."

"But there's no doors," said Mary in a panic. "I can't stay in a place like this."

"Tis all right, Mary," said Brennan grabbing her bag, "We can put a curtain up. Like those folks have done," he said, nodding down the aisle where a woman was busy putting up a makeshift privacy shield across the front of their stall.

Inside each stall was a raised sleeping platform on each side separated by a narrow bench down the middle. Each platform was approximately four feet wide, barely enough to accommodate two people. The surfaces were covered with thin cotton mattresses, no pillows.

Several hooks lined the top of the walls for clothes and hats and whatever small loose items they had. Four tin mugs and plates sat on a narrow shelf.

"Martin and I will take this side," said Brennan, tossing his backpack on one platform. "You take the other side, Mary. Maybe you'll have it all to yourself."

This, of course, was not to happen as within the hour the space was assigned to a seven-year-old girl, a spillover from a nearby family.

"All right, folks," the steward said when he arrived with the frightened young child. "This is Lily. She'll be sharing your space with you.

"Now all of you write your names down here. This will be your home for the trip. Mr. Brogan, your group of three and young Lily here are in Steerage C - Space 8. There's no swapping to be done.

"You're free to walk around the ship this evening, just so long as you stay out of the way of the crew. If I was you, however, I'd be sure one of you was always around here to keep an eye on things, if you know what I mean. If anyone goes to town tonight keep in mind we leave at first light. With or without you.

"There's 400 people I'm responsible for down here and everyone's expected to do their share with the cleaning. If you can't do it, it's your responsibility to get someone to do it for you. That includes mopping up the showers and emptying the chamber pots four times a day. I'll be posting a duty list at the end of each hall.

"Meals at 7:00 in the morning, noon and 7:00 at night. Tea at 2:30.

"There are six toilet rooms, four salt water showers and two barrels of drinking water at each end of the room. Fresh water's limited. If it's wasted, we'll portion it out. A portable kitchen will be set up half way down each hall so don't lose your cups or plates or you'll have to buy new ones. You can see me if you have any problems – but not now. I've got too much work to do. Name's Denis Murphy but you can call me Murph."

And having said that he whirled and rushed away leaving no opportunity to ask any questions.

They spent the rest of the afternoon meeting their neighbors and putting their meagre belongings away. Lily had just a small sack with her and sat on the platform with her head down and said very little. She seemed very sad and forlorn and Mary tried her best to get her to talk.

It turned out Lily only spoke Irish. She'd obviously never been to a school of any kind and must of lived in a very rural area to have escaped the 'English Spoken Only' enforcement rules.

Eventually Mary learned the family Lily came with was not her real family at all. Apparently her mother had recently died and her father lived with three older sons and could not take care of her. He had made arrangements with a family in the village to take her with them if he would pay her fare plus a little something extra for their trouble.

It may have seemed a grand idea at the time, but once on their way, the family discovered they'd made a grave error and, at this point, weren't sure what to do about it.

Later that afternoon Brennan was surprised to find a friend of his among the passengers. A fellow about his own age named Rory O'Meara, who lived in a village less than five miles from Scartaglen.

They made plans to go to a pub after dinner for a pint – a final toast to *the old sod.*

"Rory and I are going out for a pint after dinner, he said. "You keep an eye on things, Martin. I'll not be late. You and Mary can wait up for me."

"We'll be waiting," said Mary, not happy at all that he was going. Mind your pockets now. There's a rough crowd out there. I think you're foolish, for sure. I wish you wouldn't go."

"Just a pint, little sister. Be back before you know it."

6

They left around 8:00; Brennan, his friend Rory, and another young man named Brian who was traveling alone. Brian had overheard them making plans and asked to go along with them.

"Sure, Brian," said Brennan. "You're most welcome although we're not staying late."

"That's fine with me," he said. "Just a chance to get some fresh Irish air before we leave it all behind."

In great spirits the three of them walked down the boarding plank and headed toward the grimy dock area which was only a few blocks away.

It was almost dark when the sounds of raucous laughter echoed toward them from the narrow, trash-littered lanes.

The King George sat halfway down a dimly lit alley and the clink of bottles gave it away long before you could read the tilted sign, hanging from one hook. But the clientele didn't seem to mind, most of whom couldn't read anyway.

The three young men pushed their way up to the front and ordered pints of Guinness.

The poor publican looked about ready to collapse. It appeared he hadn't slowed down all day. And from the looks of the crowd, it would definitely be a long night.

The boys had discussed precautions on the way there and knew enough to keep their money out of sight and limit themselves to only two pints. They also agreed to stay no longer than 10:00 p.m.

They may have been country boys but they were well aware of the dangers that lurked in these large cities and weren't about to take any chances.

Things would have been fine if they'd stuck to their original plans. But as they finished their second pints, nursing them as long as they could, it was already time to go.

"Hold on, lads," said Brian. "It's not 10:00 yet. We've got time for one more round."

"Not me," said Rory. "Two's enough for sure."

"I'm fine as well, I am," said Brennan. "Sides, my money's spent. Let's head back."

"Well, I'll stand you both," said Brian in a slightly slurred voice they hadn't noticed before. With that he plopped a small bag of coins on the bar and shouted, "Three pints here for me and my mates."

"Come on, Brian," said Rory taking ahold of his arm. "I really don't want one. We best head back."

"What?" Brian said in loud voice, pulling his arm away. "My money's not good enough? Is that it? You won't let me stand you a pint?"

By this time the crowd was quieting down and watching the three of them with open amusement. They saw an opportunity for some fun here.

"Well, you can stand me a pint, young master!" a half-drunk sailor shouted.

"Me, too," joined in several others to the sounds of growing laughter.

"By God I will," shouted Brian to the delight and screams of the growing crowd.

"Brian!" shouted Brennan. "C'mon, let's go. We've had enough. I've gotta get back. My sis is up waiting for me."

"Well off you ladies go then," he sneered giving Brennan a shove. "I'm staying."

Caught off balance, Brennan stumbled back into two drunk dock workers, splashing Guinness over them. That's when things got crazy and fists started flying.

Immediately it turned into an out-of-control brawl. Hard fists hitting, heavy boots kicking, grimy, thick fingers gouging and thick bottles swinging.

Brennan and Rory tried to protect themselves best they could but were sorely out of their element. What had started as a good-natured crowd just joking around and having a little fun had now turned into a wild free-for-all.

By the time the dock area Gardai arrived fifteen minutes later, the melee had mostly fizzled out leaving several people, including Brennan, flat on the floor. He was out cold, a heavy ale bottle lying by his head. The rest had either disappeared or were sitting against walls. A few were stumbling around nursing swollen eyes and broken noses.

Rory's fists and lips were bleeding but other than that he was better off than expected. Brian seemed to have disappeared but he found Brennan lying on the floor and bent down trying to get him up.

"EVERYONE OUTTA HERE RIGHT NOW!" screamed a burly Garda Sergeant. "Anyone still inside here in the next 60-seconds spends the night in the tank."

With that announcement there was a rush for the door.

"Brennan! Brennan, you okay?" Rory said in a panic, pulling him into a sitting position. "C'mon. We gotta get out of here."

Brennan's head rolled and he just muttered. He tried to get to his feet but soon collapsed.

Just then a Garda tossed a glass of beer in his face and said to Rory, "Better get your mate outside, young man. "The sarge ain't kidding about the tank. Here – I'll help you get 'im on his feet."

The beer revived Brennan, but he could still hardly walk.

"Let's go, Brennan, we gotta get back to the boat. Just lean on me. I'll help you."

They stumbled outside the pub just in the nick of time and headed slowly up the now deserted lane. Brennan leaned heavily on Rory and started mumbling and pulling back to stop.

"Don't stop now, Brennan. C'mon we gotta keep moving."

"Sick," he muttered, "gonna be sick." With that he bent over and vomited over his shoes.

"Jeez, Brennan – you okay?"

"Head hurts something fierce," he muttered.

"Yeah, I bet it does," said Rory. "It's bleeding. Looks like someone whacked you with a bottle. Saw one on the floor by your head. We get back we'll clean you up. Don't wanna miss the boat."

"Brian ... where's Brian?"

"Don't know and don't care," said Rory. That little gobshite. If I see him again I swear I'll toss him off the end of the pier. He started all the trouble. Hope he's still back in the pub. Serve him right if he gets locked up and misses the boat."

It was almost 11:00 by the time they limped down the stairs into Steerage C. A few oil lanterns sputtered out smoky light revealing a handful of passengers still moving about.

"Brennan! Where you been?" said Martin jumping up to meet them. "We were scared awful you'd miss the boat."

33

Then they saw Brennan stumbling along half conscious, blood trickling down the side of his head.

"Brennan!" Mary gasped, "What happened to you? You're hurt."

"A ruckus in the pub," Rory said. "Help me get him down. I'll tell you what happened."

The three of them got him stretched out and Mary began to clean him up. He had passed out again and was softly moaning.

"Lily," she said, "get me a cup of water, will you, luv?"

Rory told them the whole story, telling them they were just ready to head back when the trouble started. He explained how it was not their fault at all and about how close they'd come to being locked up for the night and missing the boat's departure.

"I think someone hit him with a bottle. I could hardly get him to his feet. One of the Garda helped me or we wouldn't have made it back a'tall."

"Well, he's got a terrible big knot on the side of his head," Mary said. "I'll clean it up and bandage it the best I can but I think he'll need stitches."

"Let him rest for now," Rory said. "See how it looks in the morning. He'll have a headache for sure, but I think he'll be fine. He's a tough one, he is. I best get back to my group. My ma's probably worried sick about me as well. I'll see you in the morning."

"Thanks Rory," Martin said. "Don't know what Mary and I'd have done if he missed the boat. We've got you to thank for helping him."

No one got any sleep that night. Martin ended up spreading out on the floor and Mary was up several times to check on Brennan who tossed, turned and moaned pitifully all night long.

Shortly after dawn there was a lot of commotion above them and they could hear and feel a powerful low throbbing noise as huge engines started up. Soon they sensed the boat was moving. Moving away from Ireland.

They had begun their voyage.

In the morning Rory came back with his mother to see how things were going.

"This is my ma," he said. "She's done some doctoring. I told her what happened."

"Has he been like this all night?" she asked as she bent down and inspected Brennan, gently removing the bandage Mary had placed around his head.

"Yes, ma'am," said Mary. "Will he be all right?"

"Don't know, darlin'. But you did a nice job cleaning up his head. He may need stitches later but I can do that for you once the swelling's gone down a bit. Was there blood leaking from his ears last night?"

"What? From his ears?" Mary said in an alarmed voice. "There was blood but I thought it was from the cut on his head? I didn't see any in his ears. What's that mean?"

"Not sure – but it may be he's got a concussion. I hope not, but we'll just have to wait and see. There's really nothing to be done at this point. Just make him as comfortable as you can. Keep a damp cloth

35

across his head and we'll see how he does. When he starts to wake, come and get me – okay?"

"Yes, ma'am," Mary said beginning to cry. "He's my brother."

"I know he is, luv. Don't cry now. Things will turn out just fine, you'll see."

7

It took five days for Brennan to die. He never did fully regain consciousness. Rory's ma couldn't help him. Two different mid-wives couldn't help him. The Captain's personal physician couldn't help him. The lack of nourishment and inability to take in fluids combined with the growing pressure on the brain were too much, even for a young man with all his youthful stamina.

He was buried at sea, slipped below the cold, grey waters of the North Atlantic dressed in the only decent outfit he ever owned. The Captain made a rare appearance on deck to console Mary, said a few words of prayer and left shortly thereafter.

The service, if you could call it that, lasted less than five minutes. Gathered with them on the wind-swept deck were Rory and his mom, Lily and a few curious strangers. Martin placed his arms around Mary's shoulders and promised to take care of her. She never stopped crying the rest of the day.

Brennan may have been the first passenger to die but he certainly wasn't the last. Before the voyage was over, an additional 28 men, women and children would join him in a watery grave.

A couple of days of grieving passed before Mary remembered the three silver shillings her mother had sewed into the lining of Brennan's jacket.

"Martin," she wailed. "The shillings! They're gone. Ma sewed into Brennan's jacket. They were our emergency fund. Now what will we do? Will we have enough money left to buy our train tickets?"

"Shhh!" said Martin. "Not so loud! I've got them. I took them out when no one was looking and put them away – safe and sound they are. You were so distraught I didn't want to bother you. But we must be careful. We don't want anyone to know we've got that much money on us. Okay?"

"Oh, Martin," she said throwing her arms around him and giving him a big hug. "Thank you. I'd forgotten all about them. But I'm so scared. With Brennan gone, what am I gonna do?

"Don't worry, Mary. I memorized the instructions. I know what to do. I'll take care of you. I promise.

The remaining days at sea were terrible for all the travelers. The fetid air below decks was almost more than they could take. Whenever possible the hatches were opened to let in fresh air but were ordered closed at the first sign of heavy seas.

The chamber pots and shower stalls were tended to more sporadically as the days passed. Assigned duties were ignored as more and more people took to their cots, either too weak, or too ill to do their share.

Murph took Mary, Martin and Lily off the Duty List for a few days following Brennan's death, but was forced to put them back on as conditions worsened. Even young Lily was expected to do her share same as everyone else.

By this time, Murph considered Lily part of their family. Any contact between Lily and the family she boarded with became less and less frequent.

At first someone would stop by once or twice a day to see how she was getting on. Then the visits slowed down as everyone settled into their daily routines. Eventually they stopped altogether.

The meals deteriorated as the voyage continued. The potatoes became mealier. The bread became staler. The infrequent bowls of soup now had fewer vegetables and smaller and smaller scraps of questionable meat.

The hunk of cheese Uncle Francis had given them was almost gone now. Of course they shared what they had with Lily cautioning her to keep it to herself. The last thing they needed was to be hounded by other people who were by this time in 'full scavenger mode.'

The real treasure that Martin and Mary possessed was the packet of venison jerky McGuinness the game warden had passed to them the night of their going away party. By this time it was worth its weight in gold and used very sparingly.

They weren't the only ones that had brought emergency rations along. Word soon spread of a bachelor farmer who had extra carrots to barter. Another family had a sack of turnips, another potatoes. There were even three spinster sisters traveling together who had secreted a large jug of poteen in their trunk, wrapped up among their bloomers and blouses.

The only thing not available among the group, at least the group in Steerage C, was water – extra rations of fresh drinking water. For that, one had to privately negotiate with Murph who had the only locked quarters in that part of the ship.

Murph was an opportunist. He had made this trip many times and knew what to expect. From experience he had identified water as the ideal bargaining tool. His only investment had been a 50-gallon keg and the under-the-counter labor costs for getting it loaded in his quarters before shipping off.

The water was basically free as he filled it himself from a stream on the edge of town before leaving port. The only other expense was a bottle of whiskey he gave the Captain, who was well aware of his first mate's entrepreneurship and saw little harm in it.

Fresh drinking water was not an issue early on but as the days passed, water became rationed – and took on the taste of vinegar or olive oil or whatever liquid had been stored in the barrels on the last voyage.

A cup of clean, cool drinking water became more valuable than the spinster sisters' poteen. And it turned out that Murph was more than willing to provide Mary, Lily and Martin each with a brimming cup for a small hunk of their precious jerked venison.

Toward the end of the trip, most passengers spent their time listlessly laying on their bunks in various degrees of lethargy.

The oldest and the youngest fared the worst; the aged travelers with their weakened lungs suffered the most from the heat and stale air. The infants cried all day and all night, unable to understand why they were being put through such misery.

As a result everyone enjoyed very little sleep and found themselves becoming snippier and snippier with their neighbors.

Other than an occasional shouting match, outright brawls were rare. It just took too much effort and people soon realized there was no place to escape the misery so they learned to accept their lot the best they could.

Lily was a wonder. Skinny as a rail. A rat's nest of red hair. Wide-eyed and trusting. Trying so hard to help where she could. She quickly imprinted with Mary as her mother. Or big sister. Or auntie. Martin and Mary could never figure out which.

Martin had noticed that on most early, cool mornings, the two of them snuggled together for warmth. It became confusing to many of the other passengers just who she really belonged to.

She was no longer visited by the family she boarded with. It was almost as if they had long ago forgotten her. She seemed to have lost interest in them as well.

After Brennan's death, Martin had plenty of extra room on his side of the living space. They were able to move some of the Mary and Lily's sparse belongings over to his side and everyone had a little more breathing room.

Brian, the young man who had caused all the trouble that last night in the pub, never did show up. Martin asked around for him and when he finally found the cubicle where he had been assigned, the three young men staying there told him that he hadn't been seen since the night before leaving Cork. They'd just assumed he'd located other friends and moved into another steerage compartment.

Martin heard this moving around was not that uncommon – even though it was against the rules. Of course, he knew the real reason he never showed up but kept it to himself. Good riddance he thought. Whatever happened to him, he deserved.

If it hadn't been for him, Brennan would still be alive and well.

8

By the twelfth day the passengers realized they were going to survive the dreaded voyage after all. Only three or four more days to go according to Murph.

The welcome news seemed to give everyone a renewed sense of strength and purpose. Smiles finally reappeared and neighbors started to talk with each other again. Clean clothes were taken out of suitcases and hung up to remove as many wrinkles as possible. Shoes were brushed. Hair was trimmed.

Everyone knew acceptance into America was not a sure thing. Personal appearance was a major concern. They'd all heard stories of rejection slips being handed out and the unfortunate recipients being taken to detention rooms where they sat in misery, waiting for ships to take them back to Ireland.

Health problems were the most common reason for rejection. Any indication of cholera, plague, small pox, measles, just to name a few, was cause for instant rejection.

A rudimentary knowledge of English was expected, as was some proof of sufficient funds to help get started in the new country.

In many cases, having someone at the dock to vouch for them was a powerful argument to officials who may have been on the fence on whether to admit someone or not.

Martin and Mary felt confident they would have no problems. They were both in good health, looked presentable in clean clothes and had sufficient funds to get them both to Chicago. They also had a letter showing that Mary had family waiting for her there.

After Brennan's unfortunate death, Martin had revisited his options. He had originally planned to stay in New York with some distant relatives and get a job working on the railroad where he was told he'd have no problem getting hired. He now intended to see Mary safely to her destination – at least to Chicago.

Without her older brother to watch over her any longer, he felt it was his duty to take over that responsibility himself. And if he wished, he surely could find employment in Chicago as well as in New York.

Both Martin and Mary spoke very good English, unwilling benefactors of the English law in Ireland which forbade the speaking of Irish.

It was Lily they worried about. She spoke hardly a word of English. They found this very strange since it had been years that speaking Irish was forbidden by the English authorities. She'd obviously never attended any kind of school. Her lack of ability to understand the examiners' questions, let alone give proper answers was not a good way to start out.

Mary had been working with her every day and she was picking up the language much faster than expected but still had a long way to go.

Although both Mary and Martin were fluent in both languages they had been warned that this was not something to advertise, particularly when they reached New York and were questioned by the examiners.

The growing number of immigrating Irish was already a major concern to both the police as well as the politicians.

The vast majority of Irish immigrants were uneducated and lacked any kind of meaningful employment skills. Jobs that were available were low paying and physically demanding.

'Streets Paved with Gold' may have sounded good back in the old country, especially with a pint or two of Guinness under your belt – but the reality of what life was really going to be like would be be a harsh lesson to many, particularly the over-40 crowd who were planning to start over.

Nevertheless everyone was terribly excited to be going to America and would do whatever it took to make a go of it.

The alternatives were too bleak to consider.

9

Land was spotted at daybreak on the morning of the 16th day.

"AMERICA," screamed a woman jumping up and down by a porthole. "Blessed Mary! I can see land for sure. Sweet Jesus – thank you, Jesus!"

In an instant hundreds of people ran to that side of the ship to look, pushing and shoving, desperately trying to get a glimpse of the promised land.

Soon everyone was laughing and shouting and slapping each other on the back and hugging and kissing and doing a makeshift Irish jig, oblivious that the ship was taking on a noticeable list.

"BACK TO YER SPACES!" screamed Murph as he came rushing barefooted out of his room with his trousers at half mast, obviously rudely awaken.

"Get away from the portholes! Can't you see we're tipping? You'll sink the ship, you nitwits. It'll be at least four hours before we reach port and another two hours before we begin the disembarking process. And remember – steerage passengers will be the last to depart the ship."

Murph's brief tirade barely slowed the exuberance the joyful passengers felt. They did move away from the portholes but continued to squeal and scamper around like a flock of wild geese.

Now that it was official, most passengers snuck a final peek out one of the portholes and returned to their temporary quarters and got their meagre possessions stacked neatly at the entrance of their cubicles.

There was a rush to line up for one final shower although most passengers hated the thin, itchy film of salt left on their skin. By this time however, most had learned to to take a cup of drinking water and damp rag with them to wipe off most of the salty residue before toweling dry.

At breakfast Murph explained the exit procedure. He told them to remain in their assigned spaces until their number was called at which time they would neatly and quietly line up and file up the stairs leading to the deck. They would then be checked off by one of several stewards waiting there and led down into the Examination Hall.

It all sounded so calm and orderly very few passengers were prepared for the bedlam that would soon follow.

Martin and Mary were sitting in their quarters talking together softly and giving last minute assurances to Lily who would soon have to return to the family she boarded with. She sat pitifully clinging to Mary terrified she would never see her again.

"I don't want to go," she sobbed. "They don't want me. They don't know me. They don't even speak the Irish."

"Hush now, luv," said Mary, swaying with her back and forth as if rocking a baby. "Of course they want you. And soon enough you'll know each other much better. And as fast as you're learning English you'll be doing just grand."

In her heart, however, Mary worried about her. No real family of her own – a new home in a new country – so far away from Ireland. She, herself, was full of apprehension. She could only imagine the panic Lily must feel.

Soon the passengers could sense and feel a shift in motor noises. From up on deck they could hear the hustle of the crew members yelling commands back and forth.

Soon the blasts of ship horns all around them became terrifying. They were finally nearing the dock area of New York and the level of expectation shifted into high gear.

It wouldn't be long now before the ship was made fast against the pier and a group of inspectors filed on board.

First they would conduct a courteous but superficial inspection of the First and Second-Class passengers. Once that was done, they would head to an adjacent pier and into a large hall where the exhausting work of processing several hundred steerage passengers would begin.

An hour passed and the anxiety and apprehension of the steerage passengers was rising with the heat.

Suddenly one of the passengers yelled out, "What's taking so long? We want to get out of here."

Almost immediately dozens of others joined in, stamping their feet and banging their cups against the side of the ship. The yelling and complaining was getting nastier and louder.

Martin said, "Lily, you'd better go back to your group now. It sounds like it won't be too long.

"Do you want me to go with you, luv?" said Mary.

"No," said Lily. "Just give me a hug."

A few quick kisses and hugs and with tears in her eyes she grabbed her small bag and ran off to the aisle on the other side of the room.

"We'll see you in America," yelled Mary as Lily rushed off – but it was too late. She was quickly swallowed up by the crowd who were now standing outside their quarters laden down with their baggage and yelling out their frustration.

Things were about to pop!

10

Murph finally came rushing down the stairs with a look of panic in his eyes. He'd seen this happen before. He was frantically waving a clip board and his papers.

"Alright everyone," he shouted, "we're about ready. Now listen to me – just stay where you are until you near me shout out your space number.

"When you hear your number, come forward in an orderly manner and head up the stairs. Keep your group together and don't rush. We've plenty of time, for sure. We don't need any accidents at this point.

"What we've done is mix up the numbers to make it fair. We've put all 100 space numbers in a box and we'll draw them out one at a time."

"But *that's* not fair," shouted one man who was up front in one of the low numbered spaces, closest to the stairways. "We came on the ship first. We should be able to leave first."

"He's right," screamed a woman in the space next to him. "We're number three. We should be the third up the stairs ..."

Soon dozens of others were screaming out their two cents worth.

"PIPE DOWN," yelled a man halfway down the far aisle. "It sounds fair to me. 'Sides, we're all getting off today."

"He's right," yelled Murph. "You've waited 16 days. Another hour or two isn't going to kill any of you. This way, everyone's got an even chance. So let's get started."

It was obvious the majority of the passengers were not pleased. Not pleased at all. Perhaps saying *isn't going to kill any of you* was a poor choice of words.

Murph held up the box and yelled, "Here's the first number."

The crowd grew silent. All eyes were focused on him as he pulled out a piece of paper and waved it.

"Number 33," he shouted.

"YEAH!" screamed several people halfway down one of the aisles. "That's us." They immediately headed for the stairs with wide grins on their faces and luggage in their hands.

"Number 68!" Murph yelled again as the first group started up the stairs.

"HURRAH!" shouted another family from the other side of the ship as they hurried up the aisle towards the stairs.

"Number 27!" Murph yelled.

As the lucky family in space 27 started out to join the line, the man who found fault with the plan from the very first jumped to his feet.

"THE HELL WITH THIS!" he screamed. "I'm not waiting any longer." And with that, he swept out in the aisle with his family and rushed the stairs.

That's all it took.

In the next few moments the rest of the groups rushed out – bumping and shoving their way toward the stairs. It was like a dam had burst.

Martin and Mary had been watching everything that was going on from the entrance of their space which was not that far from the front of the room.

"They're acting very poorly," said Martin with disapproval as the crowd rushed toward the stairs creating an instant bottleneck.

"Let's just wait until things quiet down. No sense getting knocked all over the place."

"You're right," said Mary sitting back down on the bench. "What a mess. Wonder where Murph's at? Looks like he got swept up the stairs with the first batch."

"Don't know," said Martin. "I don't think he handled things very well."

Eventually things settled down as the bulk of the passengers were on their way. As the crowd thinned, Martin and Mary picked up their belongings and headed toward the staircase. As they passed by the far aisle Mary just happened to glance down the now vacant area.

"Oh no," she gasped, grabbing Martin's arm. "Lily's sitting back there. She's all alone."

"What?" exclaimed Martin turning to see.

They rushed down the aisle and sure enough, there was Lily sitting alone on the bench with her small bag in her lap. She was sobbing uncontrollably.

"Lily! Why are you still here?" said Mary sitting down beside her. "Where's the rest of your group?"

"They left me," she sobbed. "Told me to wait here. They ran off long ago. I was afraid to leave."

"They just left you?" Martin said in disbelief?

Lily just nodded miserably. "I told you they didn't want me. No one wants me."

"Oh no, luv," said Mary hugging her. "That's not true. *We* want you, don't we Martin?" she said glancing up at Martin with a pleading look in her eyes.

"Course we do," he said after a moment. "You can come with us."

"Really?" said Lily looking up with a glimmer of hope in her eyes. "You'll take me?"

"Yes we will," he said, smiling and looking at Mary. "Just come along. We'll sort this out, for sure. Mary, take her hand. I'll carry her bag. Let's go see America."

The crowd had quieted down by the time they reached the top of the stairs, walked out on the deck and into the lovely fresh air.

"Stay in line ... follow the others," said a man dressed in some kind of official-looking uniform. "Step lively now."

"What are we going to do about Lily?" whispered Mary to Martin as they followed the line down and into a large hall. "She has no papers. They'll send her back."

"I've been thinking about that," said Martin. "We'll tell them she's your cousin, going with us to Chicago and lost her papers somewhere in the ship. That's why we're so slow in getting here. Been looking for them and couldn't find them."

"What if they don't believe us?"

"I doubt they really care too much," said Martin. "They must be getting tired by now – talking to all these people. They'll be wanting to get home themselves. 'Sides – if they send her back who's gonna pay for that?"

"I suppose you're right," Mary said. "I didn't think of that. I couldn't bear leaving her alone anyway. Even if I had to go back with her."

"Ah Mary, you're a lovely lass, you are. You'd do that for the girl?"

"I would."

"Yes, I guess I would, too," Martin said with a sigh. "So we'll just have to talk our way into America. I'm a pretty good talker when I need to be."

"Oh, Martin," said Mary giving him a hug. "What would we do without you. I'm just scared to death."

"I didn't say I wasn't scared," said Martin, "but we can do this together. Better tell Lily what we're up to before we get to the head of the line."

Mary bent down and spoke to Lily in Irish. She told her that if anyone asked, to tell them that she was her cousin and she lost her papers somewhere on the boat. Her mother was dead and she was going to live with family in Chicago. And to smile a lot. "Do you understand what we're doing," Mary asked.

"Yes," said Lily. "We sneaking into America."

"That we are," said Martin with a grin. "And won't they be better off to have the likes of us."

11

With fearful hearts they entered the huge Immigration Hall. It was dimly lit, cavernous and bleak. Tall, dark wood walls broken up by a row of windows running around the top of each side.

As they entered, the families were directed to one of four different lines leading to each corner of the building.

There were now only five groups ahead of them and they appeared to be the last. Martin watched as each family member was given a quick physical inspection by a weary-looking nurse. At least she looked like a nurse, dressed in a soiled white uniform and constantly washing her hands in a bucket of sudsy water.

She looked like she'd rather be anywhere than where she was. She quickly peered into eyes and ears, probed into open mouths, checked for broken limbs and searched for rashes or other obvious physical ailments.

No surprises yet. All the immigrants knew this would happen. It was the next step that Martin was concerned about. It was the unsmiling, bald man sitting behind a desk looking over documents and asking questions. If they could get by him, the exit door to America was only twenty feet away.

The three of them passed through the physical inspection with no problem. With no one left behind them, the nurse quickly gathered up her things, went out the door and headed home. They waited patiently until the family ahead of them got their papers stamped and also headed toward the exit door with wide grins on all their faces.

It was their turn.

They walked up to the table. Without even looking up, the man stretched out hand.

"Papers," he said.

Martin and Mary handed him the clearance papers they received by the harbor master in Cork. Attached to them were receipts from the voyage tickets. They stood silently waiting as he skimmed through them.

"The girl's papers?" he said looking up at them and then at Lily. "Where are the girl's papers?"

"She lost them," Mary said in a quivering voice.

"*Lost* them?" he said. "How could she lose them?"

"She didn't exactly lose them," Martin said, jumping into the conversation before Mary could say any more.

Nodding at Mary he continued, "Her brother had them. I'm a friend of the family."

"Well, where's her brother?" the inspector said, staring to act a little peeved. It was late and he wanted to go home. He was starting to get a headache.

"He died, sir," said Mary. "On the boat. We buried him at sea."

"What!" exclaimed the inspector reaching for a sheaf of papers on the side of the desk. "What's his name?"

"Brennan Brogan, sir," Mary said. "He was just 20 years old and Lily's appointed guardian."

"Well now," said the inspector in a much subdued voice as he found Brennan's name on the casualty list. "I'm very sorry to hear that. Indeed I am. But I don't understand what that has to do with this young lady's papers."

"They were in his inside jacket pocket," said Martin. "We didn't realize that until later. They were buried with him at sea. It was the only nice outfit we could find at such a terrible time."

"Well, again, I've very sorry to hear of your troubles," said inspector, now visibly upset. "But

60

without papers – or a legal guardian, "I'm afraid she'll have to go back."

He reached for a sheet of paper that Martin could see was headlined "Reason For Rejection."

Mary dropped to her knees, sobbing and grasping Lily, who, sensing things were going badly, was also sobbing.

"Wait, sir," said Martin, "*I* will be her guardian. Please don't send her back. She has no family left to take her."

The inspector paused for a moment and stared at Martin. "How old are you?" he asked in a suspicious voice.

"Twenty, sir."

"I doubt that. But it's too late now to do anything about it anyway. You two can go," he said, stamping Martin and Mary's papers, "but the girl will have to stay with us tonight. Come back tomorrow and we'll see what we can do then."

Both Martin and Mary realized that if they left now, they'd never see Lily again. The ship's crew was already preparing the boat for the return trip.

"Sir, please!" Martin pleaded. "We plan to catch the train this evening to Chicago. We have family waiting there for us. We'll be gone before you know it. Please, won't you help us?"

"Look young man, it's getting late. I'm tired and have a family at home waiting for *me*. I get paid until 4:00 and it's already ten after. It would take at least an hour to get your guardianship papers ready. Come back tomorrow."

"Sir," said Martin in a desperate voice. "I can see you are a kind and Christian man. We certainly don't want to take advantage of you or your valuable time. But perhaps, if you would be willing to help us ...." As he was saying this his hand quietly slipped down to the inspector's desk and withdrew leaving a shiny silver shilling sitting there. ".... we would like to make a contribution to your church ... or any other good and just cause you would like to select."

The inspector's eyes widened and zeroed in on the coin. There sat a week's wages staring him in the face. He slowly turned his head left and right to see who might be watching. But by this time, most of the immigrants were gone and the other nurses and inspectors had either left, or were chatting among themselves and getting ready to leave.

Without looking up, he carefully slipped the coin into his pocket and said, "All right. Just stand there. Don't talk. I shouldn't be doing this."

Martin squeezed Mary's hand. Mary put her index finger up to her lips and smiled down at Lily and squeezed her hand.

It did take almost an hour but by 5:00 they were on their way, papers in hand.

"Good luck to you," shouted the inspector as they left the hall. "I prefer not seeing you again!"

12

There was a large sign just outside the Immigration Hall: THIS WAY TO TRAINS. FOUR BLOCKS.

Martin wasn't sure how long a block was. Loaded with their luggage they hurried down the busy streets. The noise and confusion was terrifying. People were rushing every which way.

Horses and carts raced down the middle. Men ran up to them offering rooms to rent. Others offered to carry their bags for them, for a price, of course. Some more aggressive were blocking their way, tugging at their clothes trying to drag them into a restaurant or a pub.

"Go away," Martin shouted at them. "Leave us alone. We're catching a train."

A policeman saw them fighting off the 'street hawks' and waved them over.

"Just off the boat, are ye?" he asked in Irish.

"Yes, officer," said Martin relieved to hear a familiar tongue. We're catching a train to Chicago. Is the station far?"

"Not a'tall," he said pointing up the street. "Block and a half will do it. Have your tickets?"

"No sir, not yet."

"But you have money to buy them with, right?"

"We have some English money," blurted out Mary."

"Ah, English money's no good here, lass. You'll have to change it into American money. Follow me, there's a place I know that can do that for you ... just on the way it is."

They followed him up to the corner and into a small dusty shop. Grimy windows let little light enter to reveal a hodgepodge of items for sale; old suitcases, shoes and boots, shovels and used clothing. He led them to the counter and said to the clerk, "Mr. Lewinsky, my friends here need to change some money. I want you to give them a fair price, hear?"

"Of course, Officer O'Conner," said the shopkeeper, a skinny unkept-looking individual who looked like he hadn't bathed in weeks. "Friends of yours are friends of mine. I'll even reduce my already meagre commission. So – young people. What do you want to change?"

"Two shillings," Martin said holding up the two remaining shiny coins.

"Two shillings?" said the shopkeeper, obviously surprised at the amount of money these young people had and now becoming a little suspicious. "And where did you get two shillings?"

"None of your business, Lewinsky!" blurted out O'Conner. "You gonna help 'em or not?"

"Yes, yes of course, Officer, 'course I will," said the shopkeeper as he shuffled to a cabinet, unlocked it and lifted out a tray filled with a confusing collection of money. "It's just that it's quite a bit of money for these three young people, it seems to me. Can't be too safe these days ...."

"Well, we're not concerned how *it seems to you*. Get along with it, man. They have a train to catch."

"Very well ... very well. Two shillings," he said while scribbling away on a grimy scrap of paper, "at $5.725 per shilling is $11.45 ... minus my minuscule 1% commission ... a special reduction for the friends of Officer O'Conner ... brings the total to $11.335 ... which I will round off to $11.34 ... because of the special friendship I have with Officer O'Con ..."

"Yeah, yeah, that's brilliant," broke in the police officer, "Just give 'em the money."

Back out on the street with a pocketful of unfamiliar coins they continued to the station.

"Now you be careful with all that money," said Officer O'Conner. "I'll take you to the station and see you find the right train. Not sure what the tickets will cost, but I'm sure you have more than enough."

"Is there a place in the station where we can send a wire?" asked Mary. "My cousin is going to meet us when we get there but I'm supposed to let him know we're on our way. I have his name and everything right here," she said pulling out the set of instructions.

"Yes, of course," said Officer O'Conner. "Shouldn't be any problem a'tall."

They soon arrived at the train station and filed inside following Officer O'Conner as closely as they could. The huge building was crowded with hundreds of people all rushing off in a dozen different directions.

Right inside the entrance was a small telegraph office with three operators clicking away in a fury. There were at least 15 people waiting in line ahead of them.

Officer O'Conner forced his way to the front of the line, flashing his badge and telling the startled customers this was an emergency.

"Up here miss." he said, motioning Mary right to the window. "Give this man the address."

"Michael Brogan, care of Murphy's Pub," Mary said, "120 6th Avenue, Chicago."

"Message?" said the clerk.

"Dear Uncle Michael. Arrived New York today. Catching the evening train to Chicago. Hope to see you tomorrow. Love Mary Brogan."

"That's it?" said the operator looking up at Mary.

"Tis," she said.

"Twenty two cents."

With O'Conner watching, Martin carefully counted out the unfamiliar money and paid the operator and they rushed out of the office. They were running out of time.

Officer O'Conner checked the train schedule signs, then stopped and asked a few people for directions and headed down one of the platforms. "Gotta hurry," he said to them. "Track 13. Last train to Chicago leaves in 15 minutes. Don't wanna spend the night around here if you can help it."

They hurried on.

There the train sat, huffing and puffing on Track 13. A large steam locomotive trailed by a mail carriage, four passenger carriages and a caboose. They rushed up to one of the railroad clerks standing there selling tickets.

"CHICAGO!" he was yelling. "LEAVING IN TEN MINUTES."

"Tickets for my three friends," said Officer O'Conner. "One Way."

"Just in time, Officer," said the clerk. "Three tickets. One way. New York to Chicago. Four dollars and fifty cents."

Martin again carefully counted out the coins under Officer O'Conner's watchful eye, paid the man, put the tickets in his pocket and gave a great sigh of relief.

"Well good luck to the three of you," said Officer O'Conner. "I've never been to Chicago, but heard it's a grand place, all right."

"Thank you, sir," said Martin shaking his hand. "You've been a big help. We're very grateful."

"Oh yes, thank you so much," said Mary giving him a big hug. "I hope the Guardai in Chicago are as nice as you are."

"Well you're most welcome, lassie," he said with a grin. "And if they aren't, you be sure to come back and tell me. And just so you know, we're called *Police* here in America."

Then he bent his huge frame way down and looked direct into Lily's smiling face and said in Irish. "And you, sweet thing, with those lovely green eyes and marvelous red hair you're bound to break the hearts of many young lads, Lord help them."

"ALL ABOARD!" yelled a porter hanging halfway out of the carriage. "ALL ABOARD FOR CHICAGO!"

"Up you go," said Officer O'Conner as he herded them to the train steps and helped Lily climb up into the carriage. "Have a safe trip," he said passing their bags up to Martin.

"I wish there was something we could do to repay you for your kindness," shouted Mary as the train slowly started to pull out of the station.

"You can say a set of beads for me," he yelled. "That would be lovely."

They waved to one another as the train slowly picked up speed and headed west.

"Three innocents," he muttered to himself as he stood watching the train leave the station. "And green as green can be. Lord only knows what they're getting themselves into."

13

It was early evening by the time the train cleared the station and chugged, rocking back and forth, along the tracks leading out of the city.

Martin grabbed a place for them in the corner of the carriage where they could spread out and relax a little. The oak benches were padded on the seats and backs but it would prove to be an uncomfortable ride, nevertheless.

The carriage was less than half full and just as on the boat, other passengers were busy staking out their territories for the 24-hour trip. Two kerosene lanterns were hanging down the middle of the carriage and were soon lighted by a colored porter.

Lily was sitting opposite Mary and staring out the window, mesmerized by the strangeness of it all.

Martin finished placing their bags in the overhead rack and plopped down next to Lily with a grunt of relief.

"Well, we've made it this far," he said with a sigh, "And I must say I'm a bit surprised."

"Yes, we've made it this far," Mary replied with a smile, "thanks to you and your quick thinking. I was terrified Lily would not make it through Immigration and we'd all be heading back home. What made you think of offering the inspector money?"

"I'd heard talk on the boat that if you got into a spot, the inspectors were open to a little 'persuasion'. It was late in the day and he was tired. And a shilling is worth a lot of money. He's only human after all."

"Well, I think you're brilliant," she said. "Come over sit by me and keep me warm. Lily's not going to last much longer anyway. She looks exhausted. We'll let her stretch out on the bench."

Martin smiled and sat next to Mary, draping his arm over her shoulder and drawing her closer to him.

The train made several jerky, half-hour stops during the night to take on water for the boiler and pick up or drop off passengers. Lily seemed to sleep through it all. Mary snuggled against Martin and later admitted she got a few hours rest. Martin got no sleep at all.

At one of the longer stops he jumped off and was able to buy a few apples and a crusty loaf of bread. They still had a little deer jerky and a bit of hard cheese so they nibbled their way west. The rail carriage also had a barrel of drinking water so they managed to get by just fine.

The real challenge was the toilet facility. At the opposite end of the carriage was a small enclosure which for all practical purposes was a two-hole outhouse on wheels. Martin used it first and came back and reported to Mary.

"There's no bottom to it a'tall. Just the tracks zipping by below you. But there are tissues for you to use."

Mary didn't believe it and had to go and check it out herself.

"You're right!" she said with a grin. "But it really didn't smell too bad. Better than on the boat for sure. Think Lily will use it?"

"She'll have to," he replied. "Twenty four hours is a long time to hold it."

"I know," said Mary. "When she wakes up, I'll take her up and show her."

"And better hold on to her hand," quipped Martin. "She may fall through and we'll never see her again."

"Martin!" laughed Mary, giving his arm a light punch. "That's a terrible thing to say."

"C'mon," he said patting the seat beside him. "Sit down and keep me warm."

At first light an elderly colored porter came through and turned off the lanterns. People were just beginning to stir in the carriage.

"How far to Chicago," asked Martin?

"Over half ways, sir," replied the porter. "Soon be stopping in Cleveland, Ohio, 'bout half hour. Plenty of time to get off and stretch your legs. Get something to eat. Take a look at the big lake. Called Erie. We goes right by."

"He's a *negro*, isn't he?" said Mary as the porter passed by. "I've never seen one before."

"Yeah," said Martin. "I saw a few back in New York. I was afraid you'd stare so I didn't say anything. I 'spect we'll see a lot more in Chicago."

"Well he didn't look like a slave," she said. "I thought all coloreds were slaves."

"Not up north," Martin said. "But down south, most are."

"Down south?" she said.

"The *states* in the south," said Martin. "Like Alabama and Mississippi and Georgia ... and lots others."

"That's terrible," said Mary.

"Tis," said Martin. "And I've heard lots of folks are upset about it."

"What are they going to do about it?" she asked.

"Not sure," said Martin. "It's none of our business. American politics. Right now we're got enough to worry about ourselves. I just hope your uncle received our wire and will be waiting for us when we get there."

By early afternoon, people were getting excited. Chicago was the next stop. Lily was wide awake by this time, her eyes heavy with effects of sleeping ten hours straight. Earlier Mary had taken her to the toilet, both surviving the strange ordeal and giggling about the experience.

Lily was again glued to the window staring out at the rural landscape passing by. This would all change in another hour or so.

14

CHICAGO - 1860

By 1850 the population in Chicago had climbed to 30,000 – a 570% increase in just ten years.

When Mary, Martin and Lily arrived in 1860 – just ten years later, the population had exploded to over 132,000 and was growing steadily every year. Over one-fifth of the people were made up of Irish immigrants.

As the train rounded the southern shore of Lake Michigan and headed north, everyone was glued to the windows. And no wonder. As the density of the city became obvious, the train left dry land and approached the city on a set of tracks laid on a levee built parallel to the shoreline.

"What in the world!" exclaimed Mary glued to the window. "We're over water."

"We are indeed," said Martin crowded next to her. "I was told it was easier and cheaper to build a levee than route trains around all the buildings and houses already surrounding the downtown area. I didn't believe it at the time. I do now.

"And what do you think, Lily?"

Lily didn't even try to respond. She just sat staring out the window, her eyes large as pie plates.

Chicago's Great Central Station was a marvel. Less than five years old, it was built facing Water St. out on a pier near Lake Michigan. The train pulled straight in off the levee.

The station was huge – over three stories tall and taking up over three square blocks. It seemed to Mary and Martin to be larger than the station in New York. It certainly appeared newer and cleaner.

As the train slowly pulled to a stop, passengers lined up to get off, laden with suitcases and packages. Martin led the way, stepping down to the platform, then reaching up to lift Lily down and finally grabbing Mary's arm as she got off.

They followed the crowd into the main hall where twice as many people were milling around waiting to meet friends and relatives.

"What's your uncle look like?" asked Martin looking over the expectant crowd.

"Not sure," said Mary. "I've only met him a few times before he came to live here. He returned home once to visit, maybe seven or eight years ago. Older ... maybe thirty or forty. Dark hair ... I think. And a beard ... maybe ...

By this time people were matching up – grabbing one another and hugging and crying. They walked slowly in front of the crowd.

"There he is!" Martin suddenly shouted. "Over there waving the sign."

Sure enough, in the middle of the crowd was a stocky, middle-aged man vigorously waving a sign that read: BRENNAN BROGAN.

Mary spotted him. "UNCLE MIKE," she screamed, waving her arms over her head. "OVER HERE!"

He saw her and broke out in a great, wide grin and pushed his way through the crowd and rushed her with open arms.

"Mary, luv," he said. "How grand it is to see you. Why you're almost a grown woman, you are. Sure I'd never have recognized you in a month of Sundays."

"So you got our wire all right?" she said.

"We did indeed," he said looking around. "Been waiting for it. Where's Brennan?"

Martin stepped up and stretched out his hand. "Mr. Brogan. I'm Martin Shannon, a friend of the family from Scartaglen. And this is Lily. We've been traveling together with Mary."

"Yes, of course," said Uncle Mike with growing confusion. "Pleased to meet you both. But where's Brennan?" he insisted.

"Brennan's dead, Uncle Mike," said Mary beginning to cry.

"What? Brennan's dead? Oh Mary, I'm so sorry to hear this. What happened?"

"Twas an accident," said Martin. "A stupid accident. He received a concussion the night before we sailed. We didn't realize how serious it was until we'd already left Cork. He lived for five days – we buried him at sea."

"Sweet Jesus, that's hard to hear. Indeed it is. But, let's wait 'til we're home. You can tell us all about it then. Your Aunt Kate is looking forward to spending some time with you before you travel on to Dubuque. And young Lily here," he said smiling down on her. "I suspect she's a part of your story?"

"She is, Uncle Mike. Will that be all right?"

"Of course it will, Mary," he said. "We can sort it all out when we get home."

They left the station and hailed one of the carriages lined up by the entrance.

"It's not far," said Uncle Mike, "but I figured you'd be tired after your trip. And with the luggage and all we'll just have a wee ride."

They trotted along the city streets while Uncle Mike gave a non-stop report of buildings, landmarks and apartments they passed along the way.

"There's the City Works building where I work," he said. "Been with 'em seven years now."

78

A two-story cement building stood on the corner. 2ND WARD - CITY WORKS read a large sign over the entrance.

"You work in that building?" Mary asked, apparently impressed.

"Well - not *in* the building. It's the headquarters. Although I'm in there every week. I'm a supervisor. I've got three crews under me. Putting in new streets and street lights and the such.

"You have a cousin on your ma's side lives down that street there," he pointed out as they trotted down past Second Avenue. "Sarah O'Neil. Not sure how you're related, but your Aunt Kate can tell you."

"Ma told me we have lots of relations in Chicago," said Mary.

"Indeed you do," said Uncle Mike. "And you'll meet most of 'em soon enough."

"Look, Mary," shouted Martin. "Murphy's Pub! That's where we sent the wire. Is that where you live, Uncle Mike?"

"No," he laughed. "Although your Aunt Kate might say otherwise. We live in a large brownstone just down the street. Our address is hard to find so we use the pub for mail and such.

"We'll stop back later, Martin. I'll introduce you around. Who knows, you might find a Shannon or two hanging around in there. Wouldn't surprise me a bit. But we'll get you all settled first ... and here we are."

The carriage pulled up in front of a sturdy-looking, two-story, narrow brick building. It was identical to

79

the ones on either side and very similar to the ones across the narrow lane.

Milling around on the steps out front was a large group of people. Every one of them was smiling and staring at the carriage. Two younger boys ran out and grabbed the reins of the horse, holding it in place. Three older boys came up and reached for their luggage.

In the middle of the crowd was a middle-aged, matronly-looking women staring at them – Aunt Kate. Her broad smiling face lit up the entire street as she came rushing down the steps toward them with arms open wide.

They had arrived.

15

"Mary Brogan!" Aunt Kate cried, enveloping Mary in her welcoming arms. "Praise God you're here safe and sound. And look at the size of you – Heavens, luv, you've grown three feet since I saw you last."

"Hello, Aunt Kate," said Mary in a muffled voice. "Ma and da send their love. I want you to meet my friends.

This is Martin Shannon and this is Lily. Martin's from Scartaglen."

"Good Heavens!" exclaimed Aunt Kate. "Be Cathleen and John Shannon your parents?"

"Yes, ma'am. They are indeed. Pleased to meet you."

"And this sweet young thing," said Aunt Kate, bending down and holding Lily out at at arm's length to get a good look at her. "Who does she belong to?"

"Well – me – I guess," stammered Martin, "or *us* perhaps," looking at Mary.

"Really?" said Aunt Kate. "Well *that* needs a bit of explaining ..."

Aunt Kate then stood erect and looked around as something important just occurred to her. "But where's Brennan?" she exclaimed. "Mary, where's your brother?"

The crowd of people were taking this all in and smiling and muttering to themselves. More and more neighbors were arriving by the minute. This was quite an unexpected neighborhood treat.

Uncle Mike went up to his wife and put his arms over her shoulder and said, "We best go inside now, Kate, darlin'. There's bad news to be heard. They'll tell us all about it in the parlor. Just the family. C'mon now, let's go inside."

Aunt Kate and Uncle Mike, their five boys, Mary, Martin and Lily filed into the house leaving behind a sorely disappointed crowd to sort things out for themselves.

A long, narrow hall passed a small sitting room on the left and a larger parlor on the right. Two small bedrooms, a tiny washroom and large kitchen took up the rear. A stairway led upstairs to the rest of the house.

They turned into the parlor where a neighbor lady was just setting out a plate of sweets and a large pot of tea.

Once settled, they got the sad news about Brennan out of the way first. Mary started but broke down almost immediately. Martin took over. It was a terrible shock to Aunt Kate who also broke out in tears, hugging Mary.

"Oh Mary, that's horrible news," said Aunt Kate. "And I suspect your poor ma and da don't know a thing about it, do they"

"No," whimpered Mary. "We haven't had the time … and weren't sure how to tell them."

"Well don't you worry about that now, luv," said Kate. "We'll sit down and get a proper letter written tomorrow. It'll break their hearts but it has to be done."

"I'll get the word out in the pub," said Uncle Mike. "There's always someone heading home for a visit who'll be willing to take a letter to two with them."

"But go back," said Aunt Kate, "and start at the beginning. How'd you get to the docks? And who's this sweet thing," she said nodding to Lily who was sitting next to Mary, staring wide-eyed at everyone.

They started at the beginning, telling about the farewell party at home and the long walk to Mallow where they spend the night with Aunt Kate's sister, Deirdre, and Uncle Francis. Then the pony and cart ride to Cork and finally the long voyage to New York.

Of course they were peppered by questions by

Kate and Mike who wanted to know everything. The five boys sat quietly and stared – mesmerized by the tale.

The second bombshell of the evening was the story of how Lily came to be with them. They could hardly believe what they were told.

"They just left her?" said Aunt Kate. "They left this sweet young thing sitting there by herself and got off the boat without her?"

"That's what happened," said Martin. "No papers or anything. They just left. She would have been sent back to Ireland if we didn't take her. She only knows the Irish. Her ma is dead and her da couldn't care for her any longer and sent her off with strangers. We didn't know what to do. We just couldn't leave her."

On hearing all this Aunt Kate started crying again and rushed over to where Lily was sitting and enveloped her in welcoming arms and began rocking her back and forth.

Poor Lily, who at best understood about five percent of what was being said, also started crying. Then the neighbor woman who had quietly retreated to the rear of the parlor with hopes of hearing the story started crying. It was quite a scene.

By nine in the evening things finally started to settle down. But that's all right. Enough information had been shared to keep the neighborhood buzzing for the next several days.

Mary and Martin did their best to field all the questions they could but it soon became apparent that they and Lily were falling asleep where they sat.

"All right now," said Aunt Kate standing up, "You poor lambs look dead on your feet so it's off to bed with you. We have plenty of space for everyone. Mary, you and Lily can have your own room upstairs. Martin, you can double up with John and Timothy down the hall. Paddy, Peter, Michael Jr. and Danny across the hall in the other bedroom with the bunk beds.

"We'll catch up on all the news from back home tomorrow so off you all go to bed now. No bellyaching!"

16

Breakfast was served early at the Brogan household.

Uncle Mike, Michael Jr. and Danny ate first and were out of the house and on their way to work before the rest were summoned to the table.

And when they came, the rest of the boys were delighted to find a 'guest spread' waiting for them, with eggs and bacon and fried potatoes along with the usual breads, jams and jellies. This dandy treat was rare and saved for special events – and special guests. The boys were thrilled.

Lily, it turned out, had never eaten an egg before – let alone a poached egg on toast. As the rest of the people at the table were eating away with abandon, she sat quietly and stared at her plate.

Mary finally noticed her discomfort and asked her, in Irish, what the problem was. With all eyes glued to them Mary explained what eggs were and how tasty they could be.

With sound effects of a clucking hen and the prop of a un-cracked egg that Aunt Kate brought in from the kitchen it was quite a spectacle for the boys.

What kind of a farm was she brought up on, Mary wondered to herself? She'd probably never seen a chicken either.

Lily tentatively took a small bite, smiled and nodded her approval.

By 8:30 the boys finished up and rushed out the door to school. During breakfast they had put up an unsuccessful attempt to stay home for the day in view of their special guests.

Their poorly-organized plan went nowhere.

So it was that Lily became an instant source of amazement and amusement to the brothers.

Although Michael Jr., age 18, and Danny, age 16, were born in Ireland, they were rather young when they immigrated to America and any Irish they once knew was long forgotten.

The younger boys, Timothy, age 14, Paddy, age 13, and Peter, age 10, were all born in Chicago.

In the Irish neighborhood where they lived, they would occasionally hear what they knew was Irish being spoken by some of the older folks but they paid little attention.

They suspected their parents knew some Irish because on a rare occasion they had heard their father mutter something that sounded like it might be Irish, particularly when he was angry. A quick warning glance from their mother put an instant end to that.

But to hear the Irish coming out of the mouth of a seven-year-old girl was a real novelty.

When the house had quieted down, Aunt Kate and Mary sat down and wrote a letter to Mary's parents. They decided it would be kinder to them, her mother in particular, if they were told Brennan was hurt by slipping and hitting his head during a fall on the ship.

Being involved in a pub brawl, even though it was not his fault, would be a difficult pill to swallow.

Martin also wrote *his* parents, assuring them he was in fine health and was writing to them from Chicago instead of New York. After telling them about Brennan's accidental death, he wrote that it was now his intention to accompany Mary safely to Iowa.

Neither Mary nor Martin brought up the subject of Lily since neither of them really knew what to say. To try and explain such a complicated situation was too overwhelming and they really didn't know how things were going to turn out.

Gratefully, Aunt Kate would later come up with a marvelous solution.

After dinner that evening Aunt Kate invited some neighbor ladies and shirttail relatives over to meet Mary and Lily. As the ladies began to arrive – crowding into the parlor – Uncle Mike decided it was time to take Martin and Michael Jr. with him to Murphy's Pub.

"I don't want you hooligans to come straggling in here late," Aunt Kate said as they lined up by the door. "Those boys are too young and innocent to be hanging out in that den of iniquity you call Murphy's. And no Guinness, mind you."

"Just one pint, m'love," said Uncle Mike with a grin. "After all Martin's already a guardian to Miss Lily. Sure he's old enough for one pint. And it would be terribly cruel to ignore Michael Jr."

"And I'll take the letters with me and try and find someone who can deliver them over to Ireland for us."

"I'll keep an eye on them, ma," said Michael Jr. "Don't you worry now."

"Get along with you, then," said Aunt Kate in mock displeasure, "and you best be back by 10:00 or I'll come looking for you meself."

"Heaven forbid," said Uncle Mike heading out the front door. "C'mon lads before she changes her mind."

Murphy's Pub was a block and a half away, down the opposite side of the street and sitting on the corner. The sounds of clinking glasses and laughter greeted them as they pushed open the door and entered into the large room already crowded with the Chicago working class.

Several small tables were scattered around the room, covered with bowls of peanuts and glasses of Guinness and surrounded with men settled in for the evening.

The floor was covered with peanut shells.

Along one wall was a dart board where four serious competitors were deep in their game. A dark oak bar in the rear spread from one side of the room to the other. Two publicans, including Murphy himself, were busy pulling pints and joking with the good-natured crowd.

Uncle Mike worked his way up to the bar while acknowledging shouts of greetings from his friends in the room.

The men sensed something was afoot. This was something different. Uncle Mike not only had Michael Jr. with him, but a stranger as well. Space was made for him by the eager men anticipating some type of excitement.

"Three of your finest pints, if you please, Mr. Murphy," Uncle Mike said in a loud voice. "We have a special guest with us this evening, for sure."

He then turned to the expectant crowd, put his muscular arms over the shoulders of the two young men, and continued. "You all know my oldest son, Michael Jr."

Cries of "Hello, young Mike" and "Good seeing you, lad" came from the grinning crowd.

"But *this* young man," continued Uncle Mike shaking Martin's shoulder, "is fresh off the boat from Ireland. I want you to meet Martin Shannon, not only from County Kerry ... but from Scartaglen ... where my own darlin' misses calls home."

Cheers and yells came from all over the room.

"Young Martin here was originally planning on stopping in New York where he had a job waiting for him on the railroad," continued Uncle Mike. "But this fine young lad changed his plans to be sure my lovely niece, Mary, had a safe trip here to visit us in Chicago before continuing on to Iowa. Her own brother, my dear nephew Brennan, died in an accident on the boat, and Martin here, promised to take his place to be sure she came to no harm."

By this time, pints of Guinness were thrust in their hands and Uncle Mike, now on a roll, continued in a loud voice, "So lads, I'm hoping you'll all join me in a toast welcoming Mr. Martin Shannon, from Scartaglen, County Kerry, to Murphy's Pub here in the glorious city of Chicago!

The crowd rose as one, raised their glasses and cheered their approval of Martin Shannon who stood there red with embarrassment but grinning from ear to ear.

In a rare display of generosity, the owner, Murphy, refused payment for the pints and joined in the toast as well. Everyone was totally shocked knowing Murphy was normally as tight as a drum.

The rest of the evening passed quickly. Everyone in the pub wanted to shake Martin's hand and wish him the best.

Uncle Mike was fortunate to find one man who was planning to return to Ireland the end of the month and promised to take the two letters with him.

Three others suspected they were somehow related to the Shannon clan but were hazy with the details. The Guinness didn't help with their memories.

Although they could have stayed in the pub all night and taken advantage of many free offers of additional rounds of Guinness, Uncle Mike knew that would have been a terrible mistake.

On the way to the pub he given the boys permission to have one pint and one pint only and told them to sip them slowly. For appearance sake he accepted one additional pint for himself but promptly at 9:45 he worked his way to the front door dragging Michael Jr. and Martin with him.

He really wasn't worried about Aunt Kate to 'coming looking for them' but you never could tell.

The lamp lighter had come and gone by this time and the streets basked in a warm golden glow.

Two rowdy dogs were chasing a hapless cat down an alley. Front porches were still dotted with families and neighbors gossiping together and winding down for the night. Frequent shouts of greetings came to the three of them as they worked their way back to the apartment.

"You know Martin," Mike said as they walked along, "If you decide to come back to Chicago, you've got a job waiting for you on one of my crews. The work's hard but steady. The pay's good and you've made some powerful friends here tonight."

"Thanks Uncle Mike," Martin said. "That's good to know. Right now I just want to get Mary safely to Iowa. I promised Brennan that much. I'm really not sure what I'm going to do after that. And there's the problem with young Lily. Not sure what to do about her either."

"Well I'll tell you something in secret right now," said Uncle Mike. "The missus and I have taken quite a shine to young Lily. I know she wants to talk to you and Mary about an idea she has. But please don't tell her I mentioned it. She'll kill me."

17

It was Saturday. Martin and Mary were planning to leave for Dubuque on Monday morning and train schedules needed to be checked and tickets purchased.

That afternoon Mary wired her brother in Dubuque and told him they'd be arriving on the packet coach Monday evening around 5:00.

She also told him about Brennan's unfortunate death at sea. She agonized on whether or not she should do it but her Aunt Kate suggested she get it out of the way now so it wouldn't be such a shock when they arrived.

James wired back that same evening confirming he'd be at the station waiting. He wrote he was terribly sad to hear about Brennan but he was very happy she was coming. And who is 'they,' he wondered?

That afternoon, Aunt Kate took Lily shopping to pick up some basic things she was lacking. She'd been appalled to discover Lily had packed only one additional dress and was alternating it with one other the entire trip.

Both had been worn and rinsed out so many times they were frayed thin and were starting to come apart at the seams. The same was true for her undergarments and stockings.

Truth be known it was her secret delight to have a young lady to shop for.

She and Mike had wanted a daughter in the worse way but it was not to happen. She dearly loved her five sons, but when Peter, the youngest, was born after a difficult delivery, the midwife told her it would be her last.

So to be able to take Lily and spend a 'girls day' shopping was simply wonderful. To Lily it was more like a miracle. It was one thing to learn she'd never eaten an egg. It was another to discover she had never had a store-bought item of any kind. Never.

Sunday found the entire tribe dressed up in their Sunday Best and heading to Saint Patrick's for Mass. Lily, of course, had never been to a Mass either, let alone inside a church of any kind. Another exciting first.

Mary and Martin were familiar with the concept but the only Mass they vaguely remembered was a rare, hit and miss affair, always held secretly in the dead of night and usually in a neighbor's barn or nearby cave whenever a priest managed to slip by the English authorities.

Saint Patrick's was already crowded when they arrived ten minutes before Mass was scheduled to begin. Sitting room was tight but they all managed to slip into one pew. Lily squeezed in between Aunt Kate and Uncle Mike who were taking great pleasure showing her off.

With her limited English, Lily understood very little of what was taking place but it was obvious she was fascinated by all the pomp and pageantry.

She was captivated by the colorful vestments of the priest, the pipe organ and mixed choir and the beautiful stained glass windows. But it was the sweet odor of incense drifting down from the altar which really captured her attention.

"What is that beautiful smell?" she whispered in Irish to Aunt Kate.

Aunt Kate bent down and whispered back, "English, Lily. Say it in English."

Lily frowned but tried. "Smell?" she said sniffing with her nose. "Pretty."

"That's incense, Lily," said Aunt Kate. "Do you like it?"

"Incense," repeated Lily smiling. "Very pretty."

"Yes, it is, dear."

Sunday dinner was at two o'clock. Despite the boy's moans and groans, Aunt Kate insisted everyone remain dressed in their church clothes as this was a special affair. Their guests would be leaving in the morning.

At the table over dessert Uncle Mike called for quiet and stood up. He had an important announcement to make.

He told Mary and Martin that he and Aunt Kate would love it if Lily could stay with them. He said the entire family had talked it over and it had been a universal agreement that a young lady in the home would make a wonderful addition.

But they realized it would be up to them ... them and Lily, of course.

Mary and Mike were not totally shocked. They had seen how much Aunt Kate had been fawning over Lily and it appeared to them that Lily had responded warmly to her motherly attention. They both realized it would definitely be in Lily's best interests.

As much as they loved her, they were both still young adults themselves and could hardly provide the stability she needed at her young age.

So it was that both Mary and Martin gratefully agreed to the arrangement ... as long as Lily agreed as well.

Then Martin told them it could present a problem as he had signed papers as her guardian. He wasn't totally sure of how legal it was as he lied a wee bit about his age.

Uncle Mike laughed and pointed out that this would be no problem as he had a lot of friends in 'city hall' that could easily set things straight.

Lily knew enough English to realize they had been talking about her. When Mary explained in Irish the situation, her eyes got wide and she looked at Aunt Kate and said, "They really want me?"

"Yes, Lily, they *really* want you."

"I'd be part of their family?" she said incredulously.

"Yes. You'd be their daughter. A real daughter."

"And the boys?" she said looking at the five of them.

"Yes. The boys, too. All of them would be your big brothers."

"But I love you and Martin," she said, starting to tear up.

"And we love you, too, Lily," said Mary giving her a hug. "But Martin and I believe this would be the best thing for you. A regular family with your own ma and da ... plus your brothers. What do you think?"

"Will I ever see you again?" said Lily.

"Of course you will, luv. Dubuque is not that far away."

"And they really want me?" she said again, turning to look at Aunt Kate who was smiling at her.

"Yes, luv. They really do."

Wiping away her tears, Lily smiled at Aunt Kate and nodded 'yes.'

Aunt Kate understood that and opened up her arms as Lily flew into them.

Aunt Kate, Uncle Mike, Mike Jr. and Lily were at the station when Martin and Mary boarded the train at 10 a.m. the next morning. The rest of the boys had said their farewells over breakfast before they left for school.

Plans were exchanged to get together again as soon as possible, perhaps over the holidays, and off they went.

In addition to the locomotive, freight car and caboose, there was just one passenger car and that was only half full.

They finally sat, already exhausted from all the excitement plus the lack of sleep the night before.

"You've got a fine aunt and uncle," Martin said. "And the boys were all great. Lily is a lucky young lass, she is. She'll have no problems with five strapping lads looking after her. That's for sure."

"Oh, but I'll miss her. I miss her *already*."

"Sure we both will," said Martin, "but she's with a *real* family now. A family that loves her and will take care of her. It's taken a big load off my mind I can tell you that. 'Sides, we'll see her again from time to time."

"I hope so," said Mary. "But now I'm worried about *you*. You've come so far out of your way to help. I don't know what I'd have done without you. Will you be going back to work on one of Uncle Mike's crews?"

"Don't know. Maybe. He'd make a good boss. There's opportunity for me, for sure. But let's get you safely to Dubuque first. That's the important thing. Then we'll worry about me."

18

DUBUQUE, IOWA
1860

Mary Brogan had two brothers. James was the oldest and Brennan had been next.

James had immigrated to America six years earlier when he was twenty-four. He came to Dubuque simply because one of his best friends, Hugh Torney, had arrived there two years before and persuaded him to come. They both knew there was no future for them in Ireland.

"Come join me in Dubuque," Hugh wrote when he heard James was saving money for the boat. "Don't stay in New York. You'll hate it there. Too many people. You'll just get lost, believe me."

James did believe him and once he arrived in New York, he just kept heading west.

Hugh got him a job working with him in one of the lumber mills in the area. Dubuque was growing fast and there was a steady demand for lumber needed for the myriad of homes and businesses that were being constructed in the area. The local hills were covered with hardwood trees along both sides of the great Mississippi River and the supplies looked endless.

The boarding house they stayed in was not fancy but the meals were well-prepared and hearty. James worked six, hard 12-hour days a week and saved his money. But he was lonely.

At first, he and Hugh would head out almost every night to one of the pubs they fancied. Just a pint or two to unwind and then back to the small, ten by sixteen-foot dorm in an area known as 'the flats' they shared with two others.

Saturday nights were a different matter. With no job to worry about the next day, more pints than usual were consumed and Hugh usually drank two to his one.

Hugh earned more money than James but managed to fritter it all away by the end of the week. James usually ended up loaning him part of his own paycheck to see him by.

Hugh was a great guy – strong as an ox, loyal and friendly to a fault but with the ambition of a groundhog.

After a month or two James realized he was headed the same direction and he didn't want that. He needed something more, but he just wasn't sure what it was – and even if he did know – how he would get it.

If he hadn't ripped his shirt helping Hugh back to his feet after a long night at Sweeney's, he may never have met Maureen Kennedy.

Main Street Emporium was popular with the day laborers, offering good prices and a wide variety of work clothing. James had mended his shirt before on several occasions but with the newest tear it was beyond repair. He stitched it up best he could, but just enough to get by. As much as he hated to spend his hard-earned money on something like clothes, he figured he had no choice.

When he entered the Emporium Monday evening Maureen was the first thing he saw and he was instantly smitten. She turned from stocking shelves when he entered and smiled and greeted him. For a moment he was tongue-tied and just stood and stared like a startled deer.

"Can I help you?" she asked again walking toward him.

"Shirt," he mumbled showing her where the collar had been ripped off and torn down the front. "I need a new shirt."

"Oh, yes I see," she said trying not to smile at the hasty repair job he had attempted. "It does look rather ruined. Come with me, men's ready-made clothes are over here."

James followed her toward the back of the store where men's dry goods were stocked. They passed by another clerk showing bolts of cloth to a couple of women.

"I don't suppose you're interested in making your own clothes," she said smiling and nodding toward the bolts of cloth as they passed. She was trying to put him at ease ... but he took her literally.

"No ma'am," he said, looking the other way as if he was invading some sensitive area.

"Maureen," she said to him. "My name's Maureen."

"Yes ma'am ... Maureen," he choked out, embarrassed. "I'm James."

"Glad to meet you James. Are you looking for a work shirt."

"I am."

"Where do you work?

"Kennedy Lumber mill."

"Right," she said reaching into a pile of denim work shirts and holding one up. "These are very popular now. Very sturdy material. This one looks like it will fit you fine. What do you think?"

"That's good. I'll take it."

"Don't you want to try it on or look at some others?" she said with surprise.

"No. I'll take this one."

"Don't you want to know what it costs?" she asked, slightly bemused at his discomfort.

"Yes. How much is it?"

"Eighty cents. Is that all right?"

"Yes. That's fine," he said handing her the money.

"All right then, I'll wrap it up for you. Is there anything else I can show you? We have several kinds of trousers ... and boots that ..."

"No. Just the shirt, thanks," he said taking the package and backing away towards the door.

"Well, thank you, James. Please come again."

He mumbled something and rushed out.

James thought about Maureen all week. He couldn't figure out why he made such a mess of things in the store. It's not like he was shy around girls. He'd had plenty of social outings before but there was something about her that stunned him.

True, she was very pretty, but he'd been around pretty girls before, as well, and hadn't acted like that. She was different somehow. He asked Hugh if he knew her.

"Maureen Kennedy?" Hugh said. "Works down at the Emporium? Sure I know her ... or about her. Everyone does. What about her?"

"She's not married, is she?" said James with alarm.

"Married?" said Hugh with a snort. "Hardly. I don't think she's ever been out with a fella before. Leastwise, with none of the fellas around here."

"How would you know that?" said James.

""Cause no one around here is brave enough to ask her out."

"Why not?" James said, confused. "Seems pleasant enough."

"Yeah. And she's also old man Kennedy's niece and he's *very* protective of her."

"Kennedy? Like in Kennedy Lumber?"

"One and the same, James lad," Hugh said. "And if you want to keep your job, I'd avoid that girl like the plague. Others have tried and they're long gone."

19

Maureen Kennedy came to Dubuque to live with her aunt and uncle after her parents were killed in a carriage accident in Chicago. She was only 12-years-old at the time and they basically raised her.

As she developed into womanhood she grew in looks and graces. They insisted on her attending school which was a rarity for women in those early days. She did well and eventually wanted to earn her own way.

She could have worked at the mill if she wanted. Her uncle would have loved that. He would have put her in the office where he could keep an eye on her.

No way! She wanted a little more freedom than that. So when she heard about an opening for a sales clerk at the Emporium, she went in for an interview and was hired on the spot.

That had been over a year ago and she loved her job. Besides two other sales clerks, there was a bookkeeper and a manager; a small but tight knit group of employees.

James returned to the Emporium the following week. He had to see her again. His lame excuse this time was to purchase a pair of socks.

She saw him come in the door and dropped what she was doing and headed off another clerk who had already started to approach him.

"Hello James. It's nice to see you again," she said smiling.

"Hello ... Maureen," he said, "I like my new shirt."

"Wonderful. It looks very nice on you. Is there something you wish to buy today?"

"I need a pair of socks," he said.

"Follow me," she said turning and heading back to the men's dry goods section again. "We have socks in black and brown. What color do you like?"

"Black would be fine. How much are they?"

"Just five cents. Is one pair enough?"

"Yes, just one pair," he said handing her the coin.

"Here you are then. Is there anything else?"

This is the moment he had planned for and he was scared to death. He stalled again and froze in panic.

"Is there anything else I can help you with?" she asked again.

"Can I walk you home?" He suddenly blurted out. "After work. Walk you home?"

"You want to walk me home ... after work?" she said.

"I do. If you'd let me," he stammered.

"But James, I don't even know you."

"I know," he said, "but I thought we could get to know each other while we walked. But if you don't want to, that's okay, I understand. I'm sorry to have bothered you. I shouldn't have taken such liberties. I'll just go and ... really sorry ..."

"I'm finished work at 6:30," she said. "You can wait for me out front. Is that all right?"

"What? 6:30?" he said. "Out front? Yes. I'll be there."

"All right then, James. You can walk me home at 6:30."

"Yes. That's grand. I'll be here ... I mean out front ... at 6:30. Thank you ... Maureen."

And with that difficult transaction out of the way, he whipped around and headed toward the door.

"James."

"Yes?"

"Your socks," she said, smiling, holding them out to him.

"Oh, sorry," he said, grabbing his socks and rushed out.

The walk home didn't take long. The Kennedy house was less than five blocks from the Emporium, up on one of the bluffs overlooking the growing business district.

Maureen realized how nervous he was and was careful to ask him questions he was comfortable with. Maureen, herself, was nervous. She knew it was rather improper to accept the invitation to have him walk her home. She really *didn't* know him but there was something about his innocence that attracted her. And he was very nice looking and polite. A far cry from most of the rough and tumble day workers in town.

She'd been approached by others before, usually by an older group of men who were drawn as much to her potential dowry as they were to her good looks. Those contacts were short-lived. Eventually they slowed to a stop, particularly with the lumber yard crowd who had learned the hard way. That was the other reason she was nervous. What would her uncle say if he found out?

The butterflies in James' stomach flew away after the first block. Once he started talking, he hardly stopped. Maureen could hardly get a word in edgewise. Finally, with less than a block to go – and the Kennedy home in sight – she stopped and turned to him and said, "James, this is far enough. I need to tell you something."

"What – did I say something wrong? I'm sorry. I know I'm talking too much ..."

"No, it's not that. I need to tell you something. I live with my aunt and uncle and he owns the lumber mill where you work. I'm afraid he very protective of me and would not take kindly to one of his workers even *talking* to me, let along walking me home. I don't want you to get into trouble because of me and ..."

"Maureen," interrupted James. "I know all about your uncle. And I don't care. If I get fired I'll just find another job. But I surely want to see you again. I hope you feel the same way."

Thus began the long, convoluted courtship of James Brogan and Maureen Kennedy.

20

Maureen was quite taken with James' insistence to see her again, regardless of the consequences. This was something quite new. Most of the other so-called suitors were easily chased off. Apparently not the case with this one.

The courtship progressed slowly. At first she allowed him to just walk her home. He was able to do this two or three times a week, as their working hours permitted.

One weekend, they arranged to meet at the city park in the center of town. Maureen picked a day when she knew her aunt and uncle were having friends over for dinner which would take up most of the afternoon.

It was the longest time they spent together and they sat on one of the park benches and talked like they'd known each other forever.

"I've not seen you at Mass," she said. "Do you not go to church?"

"Oh yes," he said. "But not every week I'm afraid. Sundays are my only days off and it seems I've always got so much to catch up on. But I've gone to St. Columbkille's a few times with my friend, Hugh Torney. Where do you go?"

"St. Bridget's," she said. "You should come and see it. It's a lovely church and they have a wonderful choir. Do you like choirs?"

"I do, indeed," he said.

"Then you should come and hear them," she said.

And so he did.

He starting going to St. Bridget's the following Sunday and spotted Maureen right away. Of course she was sitting with her aunt and uncle so they only took the opportunity to smile at each other from afar.

He always managed to sit behind them on the opposite side of the main aisle where he could study them without drawing attention to himself.

The Kennedys always sat in the same pew and arrived five minutes before service began. Her aunt seemed like a pleasant lady, well-dressed and friendly with all the people around her.

Her husband, the owner of the mill, was more reserved and spoke only when spoken to. James recognized him right away. Although Mr. Kennedy spent the majority of the day in his office, he would occasionally come out into the mill yard, usually with a wealthy client looking for some special lumber for some kind of fancy building project.

After a few weeks, James joined St. Bridget's church choir where he sang out in his wonderful, natural baritone voice.

Maureen's aunt, Lottie, soon picked up on their mutual attraction and later, at home when they were by themselves, asked her if she knew the new young man in the choir she seemed so interested in.

"Oh, auntie," said Maureen in a rush to finally get it out in the open, "I *do* know him and he's so very nice. He's been walking me home from work for a few weeks and we talk a lot. His name's James Brogan and he hasn't been in America very long. And I really like him ... he's different ... but he works at the mill and I'm afraid what uncle might do if he finds out."

For a moment, her aunt was shocked into silence.

"Well, you just let me talk to your uncle about this," Lottie said, taken aback after this surprise revelation from her niece. "If you like him so much, he *must* be special. I think I know just what to do."

Uncle Jack wasn't pleased when his wife filled him in on Maureen and James later that afternoon. He wasn't pleased at all! And when he found out James worked at his lumber mill he threatened to fire him on the spot the next day.

"You can just stop such foolish talk," Lottie responded in her no nonsense voice. "You can't keep running that poor girl's life. I trust Maureen's judgment and you should, too. If you fire that young man just because they're seeing each other, we'll lose her for sure."

"But we're responsible for her," he said, subdued after his wife's fiery reaction. "We don't even know a thing about him."

"Well, that's going to change because I'm inviting him over for dinner next Sunday!"

"Lottie!" said her husband, "Do you really think that's the best thing to do? Why don't I just ask around down in the yards ..."

"You can just hush! We're having him over for dinner, and that's that."

Maureen couldn't wait to tell James the news. She told him midweek when he stopped by the Emporium. At first he panicked but soon settled down when Maureen assured him his aunt and uncle may be strict but they surely wouldn't bite.

"But I don't even have any fancy clothes," he said. "I don't know what to wear."

"Just wear what you regularly wear to church. You look just fine and we'll have dinner right afterwards. And don't worry, Auntie is on our side."

The meal was a major success. James borrowed a new shirt from Hugh and had his dress trousers cleaned and pressed and his one pair of shoes shined the best he could.

Aunt Lottie put him at ease immediately, asking easy questions about his family and how he liked living in Dubuque.

Uncle Jack was interested in more meaty matters – like why he left Ireland in the first place – and what were his plans for the future – and what his intentions for his niece were ... (which gave cause for a collective gasp from both Maureen and Aunt Lottie).

His questions didn't faze James who handled himself well. He didn't back down and answered every question honestly and clearly. After all, they were the same questions he'd been asking himself for some time now.

The thing that put the clincher to the afternoon was when James asked Uncle's Jack's official permission to see Maureen socially. He wasn't sure if it was the necessary thing to do, but he sensed it was the *smart* thing to do. And it was.

Uncle Jack was obviously caught off guard but quickly recovered and said, "Well, I think ... perhaps ... I guess it would be all right. That is, if it's all right with my wife ... and Maureen, of course."

Uncle Jack realized way too late that he'd been soundly outmaneuvered.

James and Maureen were married within a year. The wedding was held at St. Bridget's and Hugh stood in as James' groomsman and one of Maureen's friends at the Emporium was her bridesmaid.

For a dowry, Aunt Lottie and Uncle Jack, who had no children of their own, presented them with a brand new bungalow just a short distance from where they lived.

Jack Kennedy took special interest in James when he learned from his foremen how eager James was to learn the lumber business and who seemed to have a special talent with figures.

Eventually, quietly, he arranged for James to transfer into the office where he concentrated on the financial side of the business. James was a quick study and soon made himself indispensable.

Maureen and James had their first child, a baby girl they named Roseanne, in a respectable 10 months after the marriage. It was an easy birth and mother and daughter flourished.

Peter arrived one year later. This time there were complications. It was a breech birth and although Peter was perfectly healthy, Maureen picked up an infection which weakened her terribly. The doctors assured everyone she would be fine, but she would need several weeks to fully recover and must take it very easy in the meantime.

The news struck Maureen harshly. It not only meant she had to take a leave of absence from the Emporium, but it resulted in everyone fawning over her as she were some helpless invalid.

"I hate having Aunt Lottie feel she has to do everything for me," said Maureen to James one evening.

"And now Uncle Jack's talking about hiring a full-time helper to come by every day. I'm not completely useless, you know."

"No, luv. Course you're not. We just need to be careful for awhile. Don't you worry, my sister, Mary, will be arriving soon. She'll be a big help to you, for sure."

21

Two months after Maureen and James' second child was born, Mary and Martin arrived in Dubuque.

James and Maureen were at the station to meet them while Aunt Lottie stayed at their bungalow taking care of the children.

James gave his baby sister a bear hug swinging her around in a large circle.

"Sis – you've all grown up on me," he said with a huge grin. "Six years ago it seems you were barely walking – now look at you. Here," he said turning, "meet my lovely wife, Maureen."

"Maureen!" said Mary hugging her. "I'm so glad to finally meet you. And I can't wait to meet my niece and nephew."

Then she quickly introduced Martin telling everyone that after Brennan had died, he had stepped in and made sure that she and Lily arrived safely in Chicago, before accompanying her to Dubuque.

"And who's Lily?" asked her bewildered brother.

They headed home in Uncle Jack's carriage that James had borrowed for the evening. Mary was glad she had told him about Brennan in her wire because the shock had started to wear off and they were able to fill in all the expected questions.

"Do ma and da know about Brennan?" he asked.

"I'm sure they do ... or they will very soon," Mary replied. "We sent them a letter from Chicago. Aunt Kate and Uncle Mike found someone to take it over to Ireland for us."

"Poor ma. It will be a terrible shock," he said.

"It will indeed," said Mary. "It was a terrible shock for us as well."

They were greatly amused at the story about Lily.

"Are we going to meet her someday?" asked Maureen.

"Oh, I'm sure you will," said Mary. "You'll love her as much as Martin and I do."

James was particularly impressed that Martin had so drastically changed his plans to be sure Mary arrived safely ... not only his sister, but young Lily who he was now dying to meet. He realized how difficult it would have been if they'd been traveling alone.

Mary was thrilled to meet the children, her very first nephew and niece. Her brother told her about Maureen's difficult delivery with Peter and was hoping Mary would be able to help her while she convalesced.

Mary overwhelmingly assured them she'd be delighted.

James' bungalow had been enlarged twice in the two years they'd lived there. Originally a two-bedroom, James added a nursery large enough for both children – and a comfortable sun porch they could sit on and visit with friends.

Mary was put in the second bedroom and Martin bunked out on the sun porch. It wasn't ideal, but it would work just fine until Martin decided on what he planned to do.

Martin knew he had a job waiting for him back in Chicago, but leaving Mary behind was something he no longer wanted to consider.

James and Maureen immediately sensed the budding romance between them and secretly agreed to intervene. James came up with a splendid solution.

He suggested to Martin that he could work at the lumber mill until he sorted things out. He could stay with them in the meantime, earn a little money and take his time to decide what was best.

He had talked to Mr. Kennedy the day before about a job for him in the yards and he readily agreed.

From what Mary had told the family – getting everyone through immigration and all the way to Iowa in one piece, it seemed Martin was certainly resourceful enough. And Lord knows he was stocky enough to handle any job at the mill. Perhaps this whole thing might work out after all.

The months passed quickly. Eventually Martin *did* decide to stay in Dubuque after all. New York – Chicago – Dubuque – it really didn't make that much difference where he lived as long as Mary was nearby.

It became obvious Mary felt the same about him. He was closing in on his 20th birthday by this time and she would soon be nineteen. Their budding romance was blossoming into something serious.

Martin started as an apprentice at the mill and quickly mastered whatever jobs he was assigned to. With money of his own finally coming in, he was able to move out of James' bungalow and find a comfortable rooming house within walking distance of the mill.

Mary adored her new niece and nephew and was a great help to Maureen watching the children as well as performing many of the heavier household chores.

Eventually Maureen returned to her sales job at the Emporium for three days a week. It certainly wasn't the extra income that she was looking for, it was the love of daily contact with the townsfolk that she missed so much.

By 1863 Dubuque was bustling. The population was now pushing 17,000 and work was steady for those who wanted it. The lumber business, in particular, was booming. This, of course, was great news for the Kennedy family and all employees of his lumber mill; including James Brogan and Martin Shannon.

James was now the assistant manager of the business, and Jack Kennedy's right hand man. It wasn't a position he'd married into; it was a position he honestly earned with the sweat of his brow and the quickness of his mind. In his early-thirties by this time, he'd earned the respect of all the mill workers, as well as the important businessmen of the town.

Martin had also moved up in the business. He was now a general foreman overlooking the work of twenty laborers, both in residential as well as commercial construction.

Whereas a major reason of this advancement was due to his natural abilities, an increasing part was caused by a growing attrition of mill employees who were signing up in greater numbers to serve in the Civil War, now in its second year.

News of the war was on everyone's mind in those days. What was originally thought to be a quick and decisive victory against the southern upstarts was turning out to last much longer than expected.

Although Dubuque was too far north and west to be directly affected by the war and its bloody battles, it's critical position on the banks of the Mississippi River resulted in constant reminders that a war was, indeed, going on.

Almost daily, large paddle wheel steamers would pass by, crowded with new Yankee recruits heading south. Although they seldom stopped, they would always attract crowds of people – lined up on both sides of the river – waving their hats and cheering their support.

On the riverfront itself, the prominent Dubuque shot tower was kept busy 24 hours a day, producing lead musket balls by the hundreds of thousands that were shipped to battlefields throughout the south.

Hardly a month went by that a public demonstration didn't take place in the band stand of the city park. These were festive events usually held on Sunday afternoons and featured martial music and polished, professional speakers promoting the importance of defending the Union.

Heavily-decorated soldiers in their handsome dress blues were on hand to attract the eyes of the young ladies, something that wasn't missed by the local young men.

Whenever possible these demonstrations were timed to coincide with a squad of new Dubuque recruits as they marched off in ragged unison, homemade packs on their backs and toting personal rifles, down to the river front and on to paddle wheel steamers heading south.

124

The Dubuque Herald reported the progress of the war from wires it received daily. The news was generally discouraging.

Everyone was shocked at the abilities of these rebel troops to fight like professional soldiers and frequently repel the much better-equipped Union troops.

Finally, following a major, uplifting Union victory at a remote Pennsylvania town called Gettysburg, there was a renewed surge of hope that things were finally turning in the North's favor.

Almost immediately there was a surge in the number of new recruits from the area. Enlistment posters were pasted all over town, many specifically aimed at groups such as the Germans and the Irish, the two major ethnic groups living in Dubuque.

Huge enlistment bonuses, often amounting to six months of normal pay were hard to resist. Generous monthly allowances were comparable to what a day laborer could earn. Add in a snappy new uniform, a modern rifle and competent commanders to provide whatever training was required and it came to quite a package.

And, in the case of Irish recruits, enlistment was touted as a chance to not only stamp out slavery ... but fight their English enemies at the same time.

England, desperate for southern cotton, was fearful of what was taking place as the war progressed and cotton shipments from the south slowly but surely dried up.

To many young men in Dubuque, it became an opportunity to make a name for themselves and receive that financial boost many were looking for.

Why not join now, while there was still time – was the major discussion topic among eligible young men. All those financial incentives and opportunities for glory would not last forever.

Little did anyone realize at the time was the war had barely reached the half-way point.

22

Martin was not immune to all this high-pressured pomp and circumstance going on around him. Many of his friends and fellow workers had already signed up and he was wavering.

News of instituting a draft was already being discussed and once that happened you could kiss any financial incentives goodbye.

President Lincoln was calling for more and more troops to help bring this distasteful conflict to a swift conclusion and people were finally paying attention.

When Martin mentioned his casual interest in joining to Mary, she was appalled.

"You can't be serious," she said, shocked to hear him say something like that. "Join the army? Are you daft, Martin? This is not our war. What are you thinking? Have you even considered how I feel about it?"

Martin was taken aback by her stormy reaction. He thought she'd be proud of him. He noticed how excited she became at the military meetings in the park. How loudly she clapped and cheered.

"But Mary," he said, "It's only for six months. I'll be back before you even miss me. And I'll have enough money saved for us to get married. That's what you want, isn't it?"

"Oh, I do want to marry you, Martin," she said, "although this is the first time I've heard you mention it."

"I'm sorry," he said. "You're right. I guess I've always assumed we'd get married one day. I thought you felt the same."

"I do, Martin. But there's no reason for you go off and fight in a war first. We don't need a lot of money to get married and you've already got a grand job at the mill."

"I know," he said, "and I like my job. But this way, when I get back, we can buy a little place of our own; fix it up the way we want. I don't plan to live in a boarding house forever."

"Martin," she said. "Promise me you won't do anything rash. Now that I finally got you to propose to me – I guess it was a proposal – I don't want you running off to fight in some stupid war."

"It's not a 'stupid war', Mary. You don't mean that. It's a fight against slavery. It's a fight to keep our new country together. We've talked about these things before. Remember how things were back home? We were no better than slaves ourselves to the English landholders."

"I know. You're right," she said. "It's just that we've begun setting our roots down here. Things are going well for us. I couldn't stand knowing you're off somewhere in harm's way. What if you got hurt or something ... and couldn't get home? I don't know what I'd do." She grabbed ahold of him and started crying.

"Oh, Mary," he said. "Please don't cry. Nothing's going to happen to me ... thick-headed Mick that I am."

"Martin," she pleaded. "Tell me you won't do anything until we've had a chance to talk it over some more. Promise!"

"I promise, Mary. I won't do anything rash."

The 8th Iowa Volunteer Infantry was organized in the latter part of that summer and mustered in at Davenport, Iowa, in September.

Martin and Mary agonized over what he should do for several weeks until it all came to a head when a recruitment team came to town and signed up a number of eager young men during a particularly patriotic plea.

It all became too much for Martin and he got swept up in the moment and enlisted as well.

Mary was heartbroken and cried for days. Martin did his best to assure her he would be just fine and it would only be for a short six-month period – a year at the very longest – and when he returned home they would surely be married.

Two weeks later they said their goodbyes on the banks of the Mississippi. He was about to board a paddle wheeler headed down river to Davenport.

James and Maureen were also there wishing him a safe journey and loading him down with a thick travel blanket and a heavy parcel of food.

James was very proud of him as were the others at the mill. Truth be known he might have joined himself if it hadn't been for Maureen's fragile health, that and two young children at home.

With promises of frequent letters and her favorite blue perfumed scarf tucked safely away in his pack, Mary clung to him until the last minute.

"You bring that scarf back to me, you hear?"

"I promise, Mary. Will you wait for me if I do?"

"I'll always wait for you!"

23

The paddle wheeler arrived in Davenport, Iowa, at noon the next day, slowed down by a quick stop at Clinton to take on an additional dozen recruits. It had been a miserable, sleepless night for everyone on board. The constant vibration of the boat, while trying to get comfortable sprawled out on the hard, damp deck was impossible.

Camp McClellan was a hastily-constructed, hodgepodge of leaky barracks, a parade field, mess hall, supply depot and officer's quarters. The recruits piled off the boat and scrambled up the muddy levee and into the large mess hall where they were introduced to army food for the first time.

Perhaps because it was the first meal they received in a day and a half – or the excitement of finally getting off the boat – or whatever – the young recruits were in good spirits and wolfed down hunks of greasy pork, lumpy potatoes, hard-as-a-brick biscuits and tepid, weak coffee as it were the best meal they'd ever had. Little did they realize then that it would be one of the better meals they *would* have for months to come.

After they ate they were led to Barracks B and told to grab an empty bunk, drop off their personal packs and line up at the Supply Hall to pick up their equipment and uniforms.

Afterwards they struggled back to the barracks to make up their beds, sort through and label all the new gear they received, and relax for the rest of the afternoon.

Martin was disappointed that rifles and ammunition had not been assigned to the men.

"Later," was all they were told.

So far, it had all been a blur. Training would begin in earnest in the morning.

Martin found himself surrounded by thirty-four men, all either from the city of Dubuque or surrounding farms. With the exception of three or four who must have lied about their ages because they looked way too young, and an equal number who had to be pushing forty, the majority looked to be in their twenties or early thirties. He recognized four of them and even knew their names.

Carter Langley lived in the same boarding house he did and worked for the railroad. A burly character who kept to himself, Martin was surprised to see him because he knew we was partially crippled. A train wheel had run over the end of his foot crushing three toes. Although he now walked with a slight limp it didn't seem to bother him any. Apparently it didn't bother the recruiter either who didn't hesitate to sign him up.

Banjo Porter worked at the Kennedy mill and was actually on one of the crews Martin supervised. He was a good-natured character with a smile for everyone. Perhaps a little slow but universally liked. Martin didn't even know he had signed up until they bumped into each other on the boat.

Toby Flynn and Garrett Schmidt were two recently-fired Dubuque policemen who had nasty reputations for dealing harshly with miscreants. Word on the street was they were constantly in trouble with the city for their overzealous, bad behavior. Muscular and large, they made a formidable twosome to tangle with.

It was also a mystery to everyone to see a Mick and a Kraut working together as a team. Totally unnatural most people thought.

One morning Martin had seen them come in the lumber yard looking for a board finisher after the man's wife had been badly beaten during a night of unbridled drinking. Making matters worse the nitwit suffered a terrible lack of judgement when he

133

brandished his trimming axe when Flynn and Schmidt tried to cuff him.

As might be expected it didn't go well and he ended up in the hospital for ten days. It was the last straw! Finally fired from their jobs with the police force, the army must have looked like a good solution to them.

Morning came early at Camp McClellan. It came when Corporal Quinn came charging into the barracks at the crack of dawn beating on a trash can lid with a sawed-off billiard cue.

"Up you go, laddies," he shouted. "Line up in front of the barracks in 10 minutes. If you're late, no breakfast." And on he went rushing out the side door before anyone could throw something at him.

"You awake, Banjo?" Martin said to the groaning mass on the cot next to him.

"Yeah," he said. "How could anyone sleep after that?"

"I know," laughed Martin. "I wonder if we have that to look forward to every morning?"

"Lord, I hope not," said Banjo. "If so, I'm gonna quit."

"Little late for that," Martin said with a smile. "C'mon. Let's move. I don't want to miss breakfast."

The rest of the morning was devoted to exercising and marching drills. It was comical at first to see the troop of untrained farmers and laborers stumble through the basics, constantly bumping and running into one another.

By noon some progress had been made and by and large the majority had discovered their right feet from their left and were able to start, turn and halt on command.

After a skimpy lunch of rice and beans, stale rolls and coffee, it was time for rifle practice. The men were excited. Finally they would get to shoot something which, for most, was an experience they'd never had yet.

Martin, for example, had never fired a gun of any kind in his life. The men that came from rural areas were familiar with older types of muskets used for varmints and deer. But for all, training on the new Springfield Model 1861 would be an exciting experience.

The sergeant in charge of rifle training was not patient. But he did have a loud voice.

The men were divided into groups of twelve and gathered around tables spaced in front of the firing range. Each table had one Corporal and one rifle and no ammunition.

"All right men, listen up," screamed the sergeant as he passed back and forth in front of the tables. "This afternoon, you will learn the basics about the Springfield Model 1861. You will pay attention to your trainers and learn how to hold it, how to take it apart, how to load it and how to aim it.

"Tomorrow you will learn how to fire it and how to clean it. The Model 1861 is a marvelous weapon, far superior to what the rebs are using. When we're satisfied you won't shoot yourself, you'll all receive your own personal weapon. It will be your constant companion. It will be your mistress. Treat it with respect and it will save your life. Do you all understand?"

Barely hearing a mumbling of responses he stopped and screamed in a voice loud to be heard back in Dubuque, "DO YOU UNDERSTAND?"

Startled, the men shouted back, "YES, SERGEANT!"

"All right then," he said. "Let's get started."

The next four hours were spent learning as much as they could about the rifle. Under the watchful eyes of the trainers they each took turns taking the rifle apart and putting it back together.

They learned how to load and unload the dummy ammunition and how to aim the rifle at the large bullseye targets spaced out at 100, 200 and 400 yards. By early evening they all felt they had mastered their lessons and were itching to actually shoot one. But that would have to wait until the next day.

Two more hours practicing marching around the parade grounds and they headed back to the barracks, exhausted.

"Think you're ready to shoot some rebs?" Banjo asked Martin after a tasteless dinner.

"Don't know," Martin replied. "I 'spect there's more to it than being able to take apart a rifle. Ask me again tomorrow after we've had a chance to actually shoot one. Damn thing's almost as tall as I

136

am and heavier than it looks. Must weigh ten or eleven pounds."

"Only nine," said Banjo. "I asked."

"Yeah?" said Martin. "Only nine? Tell me that after you've been lugging it around all week."

"You'll get used to it," said Banjo with a grin. "It's your mistress. Remember?"

Dawn. The second day.

Corporal Quinn came crashing through the barracks louder than the day before, screaming and beating his dreaded trash can lid. "Up you go, laddies. Time to meet your 'mistresses.' Breakfast in 10 minutes!"

Grumbling and griping, the men lined up, filed to the mess hall and ate. A thin slice of fatty ham – boiled potatoes – green beans – hard rolls and coffee. Then off they went to the firing range marching in poor fashion.

The same, loud sergeant was there waiting for them. Again they divided up into groups of twelve and surrounded the tables in front of the range where the trainers were standing beside a dozen stacked rifles and a large pile of cartridges.

"Okay men, this is it," the sergeant shouted. "Pick out a rifle and line up."

The men did as they were told.

"You are now holding your own personal weapon," he yelled. "You already know how to take it apart, load and unload it, and aim it. Pay attention to your trainers now and learn how to *fire* it. Then you'll learn how to *clean* it. Are you ready to do that?"

A few weak murmurings.

"ARE YOU READY TO DO THAT?" he bellowed.

"YES, SERGEANT!" they yelled back.

"All right then," he said with a look of distain. "My God, what a bunch of dolts we have here."

The rest of the day was spent practicing shooting. At first the recruits were so nervous only a handful of hits were recorded on the 100-yard targets. Not one hit the 200-yard targets. The trainers didn't even waste any ammunition on the further targets.

As might be expected there were a few marksmen in the group; farm boys who had learned early to hunt and were able to shoot the head off a turkey. Notations were made in their files for special attention.

Eventually everyone settled down and by midafternoon were able to hit the 100-yard targets with some degree of regularity.

The men started to act cocky until the veteran corporals pointed out that if they'd been paying attention they'd have noticed the targets were not running back at them, shooting and screaming the infamous, unsettling rebel yells.

It was late in the afternoon before they were instructed how to properly clean and oil the rifles. At dusk, they finally marched back to the barracks, half starved after skipping a noon meal, and sporting very sore shoulders from the recoil of the rifles. Most of them were also limping because of blistered feet from marching for two days in stiff, new, one-size-fits-all boots.

They were surprised to hear their basic training period was over. They would ship out in the morning.

The war was waiting for them.

Their final meal that evening was special and plentiful – venison steaks, fried catfish and cornbread pudding.

"Now that was a dandy meal," said Banjo when they were back in the barracks packing their haversacks. "Why do I have the feeling that may be the last one we'll get like that ?"

"Probably because it will be ... leastways for awhile," said Martin. "I suppose they're plain anxious to see us go."

"And that's another thing," said Banjo. "Why are we going so quickly? Don't you think two days training is a little thin?"

"Yeah," said Martin, "but I heard we're going to St. Louis for more training and topping off our outfit with more recruits.

"Think I'll write to Mary. May be a while before I get another chance."

My dearest Mary. How are you doing? Things are going just fine with me. We have finished two days training here at Davenport and are leaving tomorrow for St. Louis for more training. (We need it.) Most of these boys, including me, can't hit the broad side of a barn with these new rifles. But that will change. (It better). We have our new uniforms and rifles and I wish you could see me all dressed up looking like a real soldier. Ha. Ha.

I know several of the fellows from Dubuque. I don't know if you ever met Banjo Porter? He worked at the mill with me and is a fine fellow. A funny name, for sure. I asked him about it and all he said was his da loved banjos and was all he could think of when they asked him for a name to put on the Birth Certificate. And no, he can't play one!

The food's okay. I don't think we'll starve. Our meal tonight was special; venison, catfish and cornbread pudding. Kind of a strange combination, but we were starved and it tasted great.

It's only been a few days and I already miss you something terrible. Not sure when I'll get a chance to write again. I hope you get this letter okay.

Please write - love Martin

An early breakfast (no corporal running through the barracks banging on his trash lid this time) and the recruits headed to the levee, stumbling along with over-loaded haversacks, rifles and any other personal gear they could manage.

The steamer *Jenny Whipple* was waiting.

24

Lily came by train from Chicago to visit Mary over the Thanksgiving weekend. Although they traded letters on numerous occasions, this would be their first real visit together in several weeks. Accompanying her was her brother, Danny.

"Lily!" Mary squealed as her little friend stepped down to the platform and rushed to hug her. "How glad I am to see you, luv. And you too, Danny. How's your ma and da?"

"There're fine. They send their best."

"That's grand," said Mary. "C'mon now – let's go home. You've got some cousins to meet."

"But where's Martin?" Lily asked, looking around. "I thought he'd be here with you."

"Martin's joined the army," Mary said.

"Oh no!" exclaimed Lily. "When did he do that?"

"A long story, Lily, but we can talk more about it when we get home."

It was a wonderful weekend. Lily had long since come out of her shell of shyness and talked a mile a minute. Mary was amazed how much her English had improved and told her so.

"It's the school at St. Patrick's," Lily said. "They don't want you to speak the Irish there so I'm learning English pretty fast. Most of the nuns speak Irish but won't tolerate students speaking it at all. They say it's for our own good.

"The first few weeks were hard. Some of the boys kidded me something terrible until Timmy and Paddy had a wee talk with them."

"Well, I'm very impressed," said Mary. "I wish Martin were here to hear you. I'm sure he'd be impressed as well."

"Oh, I wish he was here, as well. Do you know where he is? Have you heard from him?"

"I got one letter shortly after he left," said Mary. "He wrote that he was doing fine. But that's been some time ago."

"He hasn't been in any battles or anything has he?"

"No, luv. Many people think the war's about over anyway. He enlisted for only six months and received a nice bonus that we're saving until he returns.

We're going to get married then and have a home of our own."

"Oh that's brilliant, Mary. I'll surely come back for that."

"Well you'd better. We'll be needing a flower girl and can't think of anyone we'd rather have than you."

Several months had now passed since Martin had left Dubuque.When he and the other recruits arrived at St. Louis little did they know they'd receive less training there than they did in Davenport. It turned out the army was just waiting to bring the regiment up to full strength.

All they did was march all day and sit around and complain all night. It was driving them nuts. They wanted to see some action.

They got their wishes soon enough.

It wasn't long after that when they were piled onto flat rail cars and travelled south to Cape Girardeau, Missouri, crossed into Kentucky and headed east toward Virginia. They were catching up to the war.

Within days they were involved in one minor skirmish after another although they seldom got to fire their rifles. The Confederates scouts, rarely seen, were taunting them and luring them deeper and deeper into their familiar home grounds.

The war, once believed to be coming to an end after the glorious victory at Gettysburg, had taken a turn for the worst.

The Battle of Chickamauga was a terrible loss to the Union forces. 58,000 Union soldiers incurred over 16,000 casualties. It demonstrated the bulldog determination of the rebel forces.

Expecting the rebels to turn and run like scared rabbits at the first sign of fighting was just a bit of silliness after all.

Martin's six-month enlistment period came and went. Much to his surprise all Eighth Regiment Iowa Volunteer Infantry enlistments were automatically extended ... indefinitely.

My Dearest Martin, Oh how I wish you were here with me. I miss you so much!

I have learned your enlistment period has been extended. I had not heard any news from you and hoped you were on your way back so I went to the local army office and was told it would be a while longer. I don't understand how they can do that – that's plain not fair! They just told me a war was going on – and that things change. How much longer? I asked them back and they would not tell me.

Lily came to visit over Thanksgiving, Danny came with her. You would hardly have recognized her. I believe she has grown a foot and now speaks English as good as anyone – and has turned into a regular 'chatter box'. I told her you had joined the army and gave her your address. I suspect you'll receive a letter from her one of these days.

Martin, I pray for your safety constantly. Please take care of yourself and hurry home. Everyone (particularly me) misses you terribly.

With deep love and affection, Mary

25

Somewhere in Virginia - 1864

Bitter April winds whipped across the southern Virginia fields now laid bare, long ago stripped clean by the half-famished Union troops as they straggled through.

The few farms they passed had already lost whatever animals the local farmers didn't have time to hide away.

After weeks of exhausting foot travel and dozens of minor skirmishes the Union troops already looked old beyond their years.

At this point it was not the ragged rebels they were chasing that was wearing them down. It was deteriorating health of green recruits not used to living under such harsh conditions.

Martin was able to put his trapping skills to use and supplemented his meagre rations with an occasional rabbit, squirrel or grouse. With the extra nourishment he was fortunate enough to keep up his strength.

Banjo, on the other hand, seemed on his last legs, constantly coughing up terrible looking phlegm. He'd lost over 30 pounds since leaving Dubuque and was having a terrible time keeping up on the non-stop marches.

Martin shared what food he could with him but could only do so much. They all desperately needed a break in the action.

Dearest Mary, I miss you so much. I finally received another letter from you (I'm told many are lost and never delivered). I'm so happy to hear about Lily. So she's now turned into a 'chatterbox?' That's hard to believe. I suspect she's growing up a bit, too. I sure look forward to seeing her again and I hope you wished her the best from me.

I am doing fine although I don't know if you'd recognize me or not. I have lost a bit of weight, and am now leaner and harder that I was when I left Dubuque. It seems we are constantly on the march, or riding a flatbed rail car going from one minor battle to another.

So far the skirmishes don't amount to much. We show up, the rebs shoot a few mini balls over our heads, we shoot a few back and in an hour or so it's over and we start chasing them again. I won't say no one's been hurt because a few have.

I don't know if you remember me writing about the two ex-police officers that left with us from Dubuque, Toby Flynn and Garrett Schmidt? A week or two ago, Toby was hit by a mini ball. His pal Garrett tied a white rag to a stick and went up to pull him back to our lines. The rebs let him get up close to his pal and then several shot at him and killed him. We couldn't believe it! Garrett was holding up a truce flag and you're not supposed to shoot at any one holding a truce flag. But I later heard we were guilty of the same thing. A bloody shame is what it is. We gave him a hasty burial before we moved on. I said a few words.

As fate would have it, his friend Toby was only shot in the arm and is recovering just fine.

Most of our casualties are caused by health issues; exhaustion, infections, frostbite and the such. My pal Banjo, for example, has been pretty sick for some time now. He says he just has a bad cold but to hear and see what he coughs up I fear he is suffering from the grippe.

Dear Mary, please continue to write. If even one letter in ten makes it through to me it will be worth it for sure. We've been told we're *joining forces with General Grant's army at a place called Spotsylvania. (What a strange name). Don't forget to keep me in your prayers. Love forever, Martin*

The Battle of the Spotsylvania Courthouse lasted from May 8th to May 21st – 13 terrible days.

By the time the Eighth Iowa Regiment arrived, the fighting had already been going on for over a week. It was at this time Martin and his mates witnessed the true horrors of battle.

Although the rebs were outnumbered almost two to one, they fought like madmen losing 13,400 troops compared to the Union's 18,400.

Yes, General Lee came out ahead in this particular battle but it became painfully obvious to him and his staff that they were losing a war of attrition.

The Union forces had what must have seemed like an endless supply of men and supplies. There was no way the Confederates could keep up.

26

Martin killed a man this day.

Although he'd fired his rifle at the rebels numerous times, it was always at a distance and there was no way of knowing for sure if he actually hit anyone. There was no question about it this time.

His squad had been positioned along a line of skimpy pine trees when a handful of enemy troops snuck up on their left flank. Suddenly, in a last ditch attempt to break through the line, the rebs rushed toward them firing and screaming their unearthly rebel yells.

One of them ran directly at Martin, fired his rifle from less than twenty feet away and nicked Martin's left ear. Undaunted he kept coming, his bayonet trained directly at Martin.

Martin had just reloaded his own weapon, turned and fired at almost point blank range. The reb, a youngster no older than sixteen or seventeen fell right at his feet.

Martin stared in horror as the young soldier, mortally wounded with a shot in the chest, stared at Martin in surprise and wetly sputtered, "Damn you Yank! You done kilt me," and closed his eyes for the last time.

In a state of shock, Martin, his own eyes blurred with tears, hurriedly reloaded his weapon with hands shaking so bad he spilt half the powder.

While Grant's troops held the high ground, later reports would declare the battle a draw.

Try telling that to the dead and dying spread out in every direction.

Martin aged five years that day. Dropping from exhaustion at dusk he slept propped up against his ailing pal Banjo who had miraculously survived as well.

It was the unnatural quiet that woke them both at dawn. "What do you see?" asked Banjo, whose eyes were almost sealed shut from discharged matter after his fever broke.

"Something I hope to never see again," said Martin as he sat up and slowly turned his head, taking in the terrible scene surrounding them.

"C'mon Banjo," he said, struggling to his feet and grabbing ahold of his friend. "We're sitting in a graveyard. We gotta get the hell outa here while we still can."

Both the Union and Confederate forces had melted away into the smoking stands of shot-splintered pine to lick their wounds and slowly, painfully regroup for another day.

During the hot and humid summer months of 1864, the Eighth Iowa Regiment continued to work its way deeper and deeper into enemy territory.

Constantly being reassigned from one command to another, its reputation as an excellent and relatively charmed fighting group had preceded them.

They were all true veterans by this time; with their initial six-month enlistment period now just a faint memory.

Counting the 35 original recruits from Dubuque and adding in 65 that joined them in St. Louis, the total number of casualties had now climbed to 38. Of those only a third were killed during fighting; the rest were so badly wounded or diseased they were shipped back home, or stuck in a festering field hospital – hopefully to recuperate and fight another day.

Martin was lucky and attributed his safety to Mary's prayers of protection ... and her blue, perfumed scarf he kept carefully secured under his jacket.

Other than missing a half-inch section of his left ear lobe shot off by a Confederate mini ball and some frost bitten toes which were a constant source of pain ... his lean, taut body had hardened like saddle leather.

Banjo was not quite as lucky. He lost part of two fingers on his left hand to frostbite and gained a set of weakened lungs that only time would heal if he managed to live long enough. Yet both men considered themselves blessed.

If there was any good news, it was that skirmishes were becoming less and less frequent.

Now they were beginning to find more and more discarded rifles, dropped in place as the rebels turned and disappeared into the woods. At first it made no sense. Why would the rebs leave their rifles behind?

The riddle was soon solved when a search of fallen Confederate troops showed empty ammunition belts.

Slowly but surely the enemy was running out of basic supplies; mini balls, powder, shoes, hard tack and salt.

They continued heading south; occasionally riding on the flat bed of a railroad car, but mainly on foot. They managed a steady ten to twenty miles a day depending on the terrain and the weather and number of skirmishes they encountered along the way.

Fall found them in South Carolina passing what was left of once elegant, old southern plantations.

Their orders were to leave all civilians alone. No pillaging, no raping, no unnecessary destruction.

Generally the rules were obeyed but as they were half starving themselves, if a chicken or goat was unfortunate enough to let its presence be known, it soon found itself in someone's cooking pot, and the locals be damned.

The deeper south they went, the more they passed slave quarters tucked in behind once elegant ... but now shabby, uncared for mansions.

Although the slaves had been emancipated for over a year by this time, there was no place for them to go even if they wanted to. And it was apparent that many didn't want to go anywhere anyway. The troops were generally met by silent, hostile stares as they passed by.

One afternoon, as they were passing a large hilly ditch, heavy with canebrake, a herd of evil-looking wild hogs broke out and scattered past the startled troops.

"What the hell!" yelled Banjo. "What are those damn things?"

"Wild pigs!" screamed Martin as he dropped to his knee and took aim. "Like bacon? Here's your chance."

All up down the line, the troops started whopping and hollering and shooting at the herd of wild hogs which by this time had discovered their deadly mistake and were swerving back toward the safety of the canebrake, snorting and squealing in well-deserved panic. Six didn't make it.

154

That evening the troops ate well. With the help of a dozen ex-slaves from a nearby plantation – locals who knew how to efficiently field dress animals – the hogs were cleaned, cut up and roasted.

The men ate their fill, smoked what they could, and gave the rest to the plantation workers.

This time there were plenty of smiles to go around.

My sweet Martin - I was about ready to give up on you when a second letter arrived this morning ... months after it was written. What in the world? I was terribly sad to hear about the death of that Dubuque policeman. I have sent off several letters of my own and have to assume they are taking a long time to reach you as well. Anyway I was most pleased to hear from you although by now I am certain you are miles and miles away.

We hear the war is taking longer than expected although the news is generally favorable. I pray for your safety every evening when I go to bed and am keeping a very positive attitude.

Things here at home are about the same. Maureen seems like she has regained all her strength and is working three days a week at the Emporium. I am still watching the kids and loving it. But I miss you terribly - Please write when you can.

Your Mary

27

The winter months arrived with a vengeance. Bitter wet winds blew in from the gulf coast as the troops crossed into Georgia chasing pesky pockets of Confederate troops that spent their time attacking Union supply lines, tearing up miles of railroad track and cutting down telegraph wires; anything they could possibly do to slow down the relentless advance of the Union Army.

"I thought it'd be warmer than this down south," said Banjo, shivering under a skimpy blanket one night.

"Me as well," replied Martin as he fed scraps of wood into their camp fire. "I've got a bit of coffee left. I'll boil it up for us. Give us a bit of warmth, it will."

"That'll be good," said Banjo. "I don't know what I'd do without you, Martin. You've been a good friend to me."

"As you would be to me, I'm sure," said Martin.

"Do you miss home?" said Banjo.

"You mean Ireland?" said Martin. "Or Dubuque?"

"Both, I guess," Banjo replied. "But mainly I was talking about Ireland."

"I miss the good parts," said Martin. "I miss my ma and da, for sure. And my sister, Colleen.

"And I miss the green land and salty breeze, as well. But I don't miss the dead-end feeling everyone had. And the lack of freedom living under the English. That's why I left to come to America in the first place. How about you?"

"I was born here," said Banjo. "Right in Iowa. So were my folks. Not sure about my grand folks. But I know what you mean. All I know is farming ... until I went to work at the mill.

"I've got five brothers and sisters living at home. Had to get away. They didn't need me on the farm anyway. It's not that big. I really had no opportunity to go anywhere. This soldiering is like learning a new trade, although I'll be glad when it's over. We'll both have money in our pockets then. Lots of new opportunities for both of us."

"Yeah," said Martin, "that's why I joined. I plan to get married as soon as I get home. The money will help Mary and me build a house. But that wasn't the only reason. A big part was this slavery problem. That's just wrong! It's worse than living under the English. I guess I'm surprised these rebs are willing to die to protect it. Not sure I'll ever understand that."

"Is that blue scarf I've seen you sneak out and sniff every once and awhile from Mary?"

"Tis. It keeps me going sometimes, that's for sure."

My Dear Martin -

Mary told us you joined the army. I was heartbroken to hear the news but I can't say I was too surprised. Michael Jr. joined just last month and has already gone south somewheres. Michael and Kate are very proud of him and took him down to Murphy's Pub where he was toasted by all the boyos there. I may not be surprised, but I am worried sick for both of you and pray for you every night. You will always be very special to me, Martin, you and Mary, for helping me come to America. I am very, very happy here and love my new family.

I have made friends with lots of my class mates. Although most of them are from Irish families, there are a few who have German parents and speak with an accent just like me. So, now I don't feel so different any more. Besides, the Sisters say we are all children of God and treat us all the same.

I know you're probably very busy and don't have a lot of free time but I would love to receive a letter from you.

Lots and Lots of Love - Lily

By early spring of 1865 the Iowa Eighth Infantry was now carrying the name: *Veteran* Volunteers, a new designation recognizing their long-term commitment to the cause.

They had now been assigned to General Canby's Sixteenth Army Corps and were amassing in southern Alabama around the eastern shores of Mobile Bay – in an area known as Spanish Fort.

Dating back to 1712 when it was originally a French trading post near Mobile, Spanish Fort had since morphed into a strategic location in the protection of Mobile Bay.

Sitting high on a steep bluff, Fort Blakeley was a fearsome place, bristling with cannon and packed with determined Confederate troops. Heavily defended against attacks from behind, it sat looking down on the bay, effectively protecting the city from invasion of Union troops by water.

The fort had to be taken and the Iowa Eighth Veteran Volunteers were destined to play a key part in the assault.

Martin's life was about to change forever.

28

Mary dearest - I have not heard from you in awhile but I'm sure your letters will catch up with us soon. But good news! I did receive a letter a few weeks ago from Lily. What a great surprise. She sounds so grown up. I shutter to think of her almost being sent back on the boat to Ireland. The good Lord was surely looking over us that day.

We have been on the move, for sure, rushing from place to place. We are way down in southern Alabama right now and preparing for a big fight tomorrow. I hope it's the last one. We hear the war is about over (of course we've heard that before but I believe it may be true this time). The rebs seem to be getting more desperate and we know they are running out of supplies since we're finding more and more discarded rifles because they don't have enough ammunition to go around (good news for us). My friend, Banjo, is feeling much better now, I'm happy to say. Like me he really misses home.

Mary, I count the days before we meet again. I miss you so very much. My sincere love ... Martin

The Union troops advanced slowly from the east. The area was an almost impenetrable maze of pine trees, vast swampy lowlands and thick, thorny underbrush.

The rebs knew they were coming. And they had the advantage. This was their home ground. They knew the terrain well and had placed trained snipers in trees watching from afar.

The swampy areas made any kind of advancement dangerous and miserable. If there was any consolation, it was that the weather was cool enough to keep snakes at bay. They were still everywhere but sluggish in the cool temperatures.

"I hate snakes," Martin said to Banjo one day. "We don't have snakes in Ireland. Blessed St. Patrick took care of that."

"Well there are plenty to go around down here," Banjo said. "Water Moccasins love these swampy areas. We don't have Moccasins up in Iowa but there

are plenty of Rattlesnakes in the bluffs back home –
and there're just as bad. Maybe worse. Best watch
your step, Martin."

"Snakes on the ground and snipers in the trees,"
Martin said. "Are we safe anywhere?"

The rebs knew if they lost Fort Blakeley they would
lose Mobile. It was a realization they could not abide.

But the Union troops kept coming, slowly,
relentlessly. A week of frantic fighting passed and
they were now close enough to hear the cannons at
the Fort firing down on Union ships trying to fight
their way through the blockade.

By this time they had their own cannons being
dragged overland behind them. They would soon be
near enough to bombard the fort from the rear. With
shells coming at them from ships in the bay and now
from the rear the rebs' days were numbered.

Martin and Banjo, along with a dozen more Iowa
veterans had maneuvered themselves onto one of
higher hills and could now actually see the enemy
fort for the first time.

Over their heads their own cannon shells began
systemically falling on the enemy.

Hundreds of Confederate troops were digging
trenches between them and the fort. It looked like a
suicide situation to Martin. The ground was already
littered with wounded and dying Confederate troops.

"What are they thinking?" Martin muttered as he
fired down on them, reloading and firing as quickly
as possible. "Why don't they surrender? They have

no chance. Looks like half the fort has already been blown away."

"They're a brave bunch, for sure," said Banjo, "but they won't last another day."

And then – catastrophe struck!

Martin and his mates heard the dreaded whistle sound coming just seconds before the shell landed among them and the hill top they were on disappeared. It was a short round from one of their own cannons that hit them. A faulty fuse caused the fatal problem.

Four soldiers were killed instantly, only partially identifable. Five were badly wounded and survival for them looked grim.

Two escaped unscathed; an unexplained miracle.

Banjo's left arm was shattered at the elbow by a hunk of hot iron. He also suffered other multiple cuts and abrasions.

Martin was literally blown sky high and landed thirty feet away, unconscious and semi naked. He was half buried in dirt and debris and suffered ruptured eardrums, a shredded back, torn scalp, dislocated shoulder, and a concussion.

Ironically, about the exact same time the short round landed on Martin's squad at Spanish Fort, General Robert E. Lee formally surrendered his Confederate Army of Northern Virginia to General Ulysses S. Grant's Federal Army of the Potomac at Appomattox Court House in Virginia some 700 miles away.

The death knell for the south had been rung. For all practical purposes the Civil War was over although it would be several weeks before telegraph lines were repaired and the word spread.

As Banjo predicted, Fort Blakeley fell shortly after noon the following day. The Confederate troops that survived the battle and were still able to walk scattered to fight another day.

After hearing the news about Fort Blakeley, the city of Mobile immediately surrendered to prevent any further destruction to the town.

The last major battle of the civil war was finally over. Now came the time to clean up what was left of the aftermath.

As the Union fighting forces swept northwards to chase the fleeing Confederates, the special medical squads were brought up from the rear.

Weary doctors and nurses and field-tested attendants patched up the wounded as best they could; returning some to their outfits, sending others to field hospitals for repair and recuperation, and if they were lucky enough to survive the cure, to be later sent home or back to the field.

As soon as possible these medical teams followed the path of the Union forces north, ready to jump in again after the next battle or skirmish took place.

Banjo was considered fixable. They slapped a tourniquet on his arm, laid him in the back of a wagon and dropped him off at a hastily set up field hospital near Mobile.

Drifting in and out of consciousness he lay on a soiled pallet outside the operating tent for a day and a half before the exhausted doctors and nurses could even see him. By that time it was too late to save the arm.

Perhaps if he had been lucky enough to have been seen by a skilled surgeon who had the right tools and ample time, the arm could have been patched together. Unfortunately this was a war zone, not a big city hospital. By the time the medical team got to him he was allowed less than a minute for triage.

"Cut it and sew it," was the decision made by a field doctor dead on his feet with a throbbing back and bloodshot eyes.

So the severed arm joined a growing pile of limbs which would be unceremoniously burned at the end of the day.

Back at the site of the battle, it was time for the grisly work to begin.

First came squads of negro laborers to collect the corpses and parts thereof. It didn't make any difference at this point, Union and Confederate were lined up for speedy burials. No final words, no services of any kind. Just a shallow hole ... and as quickly as possible.

Finally, as dusk settled on the still smoldering battle grounds the local scavengers crept in. They were expected. It was just a part of the scene of war. They would never molest the hastily buried bodies. If caught doing that they knew they would be instantly hanged – man, woman or child.

There were always discarded items of some worth to be found; a misplaced boot or other piece of clothing, food packets, canteens and belts, shovels and picks, and if one were lucky, a pistol, rifle or bayonet left sticking up out of the mounds of dirt or trampled in the ditches.

Anything that could be eaten, drank, worn or bartered for basic supplies was the goal.

It was a matter of survival for the ones who remained behind.

29

Martin was found late the next afternoon. He was barely alive. The only part of his body showing through the dirt and strewn foliage was his right hand and foot and a part of his face although you would have to get close to recognize what you were looking at.

Boon Taylor, a six-year-old negro boy spied his boot sticking up out of the dirt and ran and grabbed for it before anyone else did. He had no idea a foot was still inside it.

When he pulled at the boot and started to uncover a leg, he immediately jumped back. Slowly his eyes passed over the mound of debris and spotted a hand, finally a face. Boon jumped to his feet and ran off screaming for his ma.

The rest of the Taylor clan were close by and came running.

"There ma," said Boon pointing to the heap in the dirt."

"Back off now, Boon," said Tanya Taylor, his mother. "Let me look."

She carefully began to brush off the dirt around Martin's boot exposing his leg. Next she brushed off his hand and arm and carefully worked her way up toward his head. Too fearful to touch his body she was using a snapped off tree branch to brush the debris from around his face.

"Good Lord, they missed this one," she said.

Suddenly Martin's eyes flew open and a deep moan came out of his mouth.

She instantly jumped back and screamed, "Sweet Jesus. This boy ain't dead yet!"

Before long a small group gathered around watching, mesmerized as Martin's entire body was carefully uncovered with all his limbs appearing intact.

"What you gonna do now?" said Toby, her husband. "Looks like a goner. We get in trouble they come back and find us. Best leave 'im be and get outta here."

"Can't just leave 'im," said Tanya. "He die for sure. He been lying up here for two days now. Must be terrible thirsty."

She bent back down and said, "Boy, you thirsty? Want some water?"

Martin was fading into and out of consciousness and his eyes were opening and closing slowly but stayed focused on her face.

"Water?" she said again. "You thirsty?"

Martin looked at her and grimaced. He tried to move but only groaned. He looked confused and licked his grimy lips.

"Can you hear me?" she said louder. "You want some water?" She then pantomimed drinking from a cup.

Martin's eyes opened wide and he tried to move his head up and down.

"Boon, run fetch some water."

When Boon rushed back with a dipper full she put it to his lips. Martin started gulping it frantically, spilling most of it down his chest.

"He be thirsty all right. More water, Boon."

Martin struggled a little as if he were trying to get up.

"Help me sit 'im up, Toby," she said.

As they started to lift Martin into a sitting position he screamed out in agony and passed out again.

"Oh Sweet Jesus," she said. "Look at his shoulder. It's out! And his back all cut up and burnt. Got a rip across the back of his head, too. Someone go fetch Miss Lorraine."

Miss Lorraine DeBoines was a seventy-something, tiny slip of a woman who lived alone in a one room

169

shack in the bayou. The only surviving child of a Cajun gator hunter and a negro slave from Ghana, she inherited a mix of strange talents from them both; one of these talents was a skill with healing.

She was feared by almost everyone in the area, especially the children who all believed she possessed the *evil eye*. None of the grownups were very comfortable having her around either but in the case of medical emergencies like this she was the last ditch hope.

Within an hour Miss Lorraine arrived at the scene with a bag of homemade remedies including a selection of foul smelling salves, bottles of mysterious potions, a length of rope and strips of bandages. She came prepared after hearing what she'd find.

After a quick inspection of Martin and his problems she said, "Shoulder out all right. Gotta get it back. Gonna hurt. Need three strong men; one on each leg, one on the arm."

The men quickly got into position. Toby, a brute of a man was assigned to the arm, two others gripped the legs. Miss Lorraine checked everyone's position, making adjustments, while Martin, now semi awake again, looked in panic at the people clinging to him.

"When I tell you," said Miss Lorraine, ignoring Martin and looking at the men holding each leg, "you two hold on tight and Toby, you pull hard."

"Ready? All right, PULL!"

The sound of the shoulder snapping back into place was almost as loud as Martin's scream. Mercifully, he passed out again.

"Good," she said. "Set 'im up and wash that back while he's still out."

Tanya and two other ladies carefully washed his back, rinsing the dirt out of the cuts and avoiding the burn marks as much as possible.

Miss Lorraine opened her tins of salve and began smearing the foul-smelling ointments over the burns. Then she used another salve and wiped down the cuts.

Next she began wrapping the shoulder tightly, continuing the muslin around his chest all the way down to his waist where a belt held up what was left of his shredded pants.

A quick inspection below his waist and Miss Lorraine announced, "Boy's lucky. Got all his parts – but soiled hisself. Legs bruised bad, too. Wash 'im up and take off that boot. Wonder where the other's gone? I'm gonna shave his head back here ... looks like he be scalped or something."

An hour and a half later and they were all done. By this time Martin was beginning to come around again, head slowly moving side to side and moaning.

"Boy's gonna hurt some," Miss Lorraine said reaching for one of her potion bottles and lifting it to Martin's mouth. "This will help. Make 'im sleep, too."

She dribbled some of the liquid into his mouth, rubbed his throat and waited until he swallowed.

Almost instantly he fell back, totally unconscious.

171

"What you gonna do with 'im now?" she said, looking at Toby.

"Don't be looking at me," Toby said with alarm. "Ain't mine."

"Boy needs tending," Miss Lorraine said. "Leave 'im here and he die. What you think Tanya?"

All eyes turned to Tanya.

"Well," Tanya said tentatively, "can't let 'im die. We found 'im. 'Spect we can watch 'im for awhile."

Miss Lorraine said, "Keep 'im quiet. Here's a bit of salve and potion. Don't need much. A long rest is best for 'im. I'll come by in a few days to check on him ... change the bandage.

"He gets the fever, mix a pinch of this in a cup of water." She handed Tanya a palm parcel with some brown powder in it.

Toby groaned, obviously upset, "What you thinking, Tanya? How's this gonna work? We already got three chillun of our own."

"We'll manage somehow," she said. "C'mon, let's fetch 'im home."

30

The first week was the worse. They placed Martin on a cane pallet outside their two-room wood shanty; adjacent to their outside kitchen. Toby and Tanya had one small room to themselves. The three children, Burwell, age 10, Charlotte, age eight and Boon, age six, shared the other room with a rickety table and two benches.

For two days Martin faded into and out of consciousness and moaned continuously. Tanya gave him all the water he could keep down occasionally laced with a little of Miss Lorraine's secret potion.

On the third day, he started to develop a high fever and chills. Tanya, as directed by Miss Lorraine, mixed a pinch of the brown powder in a cup of water and helped him drink it down. Whatever it was, it worked and he soon fell into a deep sleep.

The next day Martin turned the corner. He woke with the sun and stayed awake most of the day and he said his first words.

It was at this point, however, Tanya discovered he had more problems. For one thing he couldn't hear.

Tanya was spooning in his first solid food in several days; a bowl of fish soup and hunk of corn bread. "Eat slow now," she said. "You be sick you eat too fast."

"More please," Martin croaked out. "More!"

"I says eat slow!" Tanya said. "You hear me?"

Martin ignored her and wolfed down the food as fast as he could, coughing and choking.

"More, please," he said again, pointing to his mouth. Suddenly he froze as he realized he could not hear his own voice. He looked at Tanya and said, "Can you hear me?"

"Yes, boy. I hears you. You hear me?"

He looked at her moving mouth and shook his head 'no'.

Miss Lorraine came the next week to see how things were going. Tanya told her that Martin couldn't hear.

"'Fraid the boy's deaf!" she said.

Miss Lorraine looked in his ears and started talking very loudly close to his ears.

"Hear?" she said.

Martin knew what she was doing and shook his head.

She reached into her mysterious bag and withdrew an old goat bell. She put the bell right up against his right ear and struck it with a metal rod.

Instantly Martin smiled and said, "I can hear that. Just a little ..."

She tested the other ear and had the same positive result.

"He be all right," she announced to Tanya. "Take time though. Don't know how long. Many days I 'pose. Little by little he hear more."

She then poured a few drops of a greenish-looking liquid into each ear and gently pushed in dabs of cotton.

"Keep dry," she told Tanya. "Leave cotton in three days. Will help."

Overall Miss Lorraine seemed very pleased to see Martin up and slowly hobbling around. She changed the dressing on his back and head and looked his shoulder over. A few pokes here, a few pokes there and she seemed satisfied.

"I be back," she said and left, walking into the woods without glancing back.

Although no one could say for sure, there appeared to be a very large animal, almost like a black bear, waiting for her just inside the tree line. No one ever considered following her to find out.

Martin spent the next month recuperating. The bluish-yellow bruises on his legs and hips slowly faded. His shoulder was still very tender but getting more flexible day by day. The burns and cuts on his back and head were healing nicely.

The scalp wound healed the slowest ... a shallow swath an inch wide and three inches long. Luckily it wasn't deep. In time the hair grew back but came in pure white.

Every day he could hear a little better and the family no longer had to shout to make themselves heard.

He would often leave with the children and go for long walks through the swampy woods. They taught him where to fish in the nearby streams and how to avoid the Water Moccasins when he went to bathe. They pointed out where the wild onions and carrots grew.

He taught them how to make and set snares for small animals and how to quickly skin them and smoke the meat.

When he discovered none of them could read nor write he took great pains trying to teach them. He'd scratch the alphabet out in the dirt of the yard, letter by letter.

It went slowly at first, but when he started doing their names it was like a light switched on. Then they were like little sponges soaking up the lessons almost as fast as he taught them.

Tanya watched from afar and smiled.

Their community, if you could call it that, was very small. Everyone was self-supporting as they lived several miles from any towns or villages.

Of course all the neighbors were quite curious about Martin and would occasionally stop by Tanya's with some fresh vegetables – or a jar of preserves. Martin would aways take time to smile and say hello.

He spent at least an hour every day tending their small garden; pulling weeds, picking okra and beans, planting greens. It freed Tanya up for other tasks and even Toby came to appreciate his help.

Miss Lorraine came again one afternoon and removed the bandages for the last time. Before she left, she gave him a soiled blue scarf.

"What's this?" he asked.

"Don't know, but must be something. You had it tight in your fist the day we found you. Good medicine I think."

Tanya asked how he was doing.

"He be marked but looks passable," Miss Loraine said. "Let the sun and air finish. Be well enough to go home soon."

If only he knew where home was.

31

Martin realized his memory was gone the day Tanya asked him his name. He looked at her with a blank face.

She thought he couldn't hear her so she asked again in a louder voice.

"My name Tanya. Who are you?"

"I heard you," he said. "I'm just trying to remember. I'm pretty sure my name is Martin ... Martin Shannon. But I can't remember any more than that."

For some time Martin had suspected something was wrong but was avoiding the issue. At first he thought it was a temporary thing, somehow connected with his loss of hearing. He hoped he would soon remember things; little by little, like regaining his hearing – slowly but surely.

But it didn't happen. He was pretty sure of his name. But where he lived. His family and friends. How old he was. Where he was born. How he got to Alabama. The blue scarf. Nothing.

He asked Tanya lots of questions, but she couldn't help him much. She told him he was a soldier from somewheres up north. She didn't know where. She told him he was with lots of soldiers and had fought nearby in a big battle at a place called Spanish Fort – but she didn't know why.

"Where are the others?" he asked. "Why am I still here?"

"They gone and moved back north," she said. "Some got kilt and buried. They leave you behind 'cause you be covered in dirt and stuff. Didn't know you was still here. Boon found you days later.

"Anyways," she said, "heard the fightings all over now. I 'spect they all be home. 'spect you will too one of these days."

With his Irish accent Tanya and the rest of the family knew Martin talked funny. But since they'd never talked to a white person from the north before, they thought all Yankees talked that way.

She'd bring it up with Miss Lorraine next time she came calling. Miss Lorraine talked funny, too.

By late June, Martin was growing restless. The weather was turning quickly and like a migrating bird, he sensed it was time to leave.

He'd been with Tanya's family for almost three months by this time. He realized he couldn't stay for ever.

He knew which direction to go. Tanya had shown him how to study the sky at night and find the North Star.

"You go north, Martin. Follow the drinking gourd. Find your home."

Physically he was in very good shape. Tanned like a berry, heavily bearded and with a flat hard stomach, he'd never felt so healthy.

Except for a slight limp in his left leg that would stay with him the rest of his life, a notch out of one ear, and a back crisscrossed with burned tissue and shrapnel scars, he was in decent shape. And the stripe of white hair. Don't forget about that.

At least he'd survived this far.

He announced his pending departure to the family over a dinner of crawfish gumbo and cornbread he had made himself with a little help from their daughter, Charlotte.

He told them he was planning to leave the following week.

Tanya spread the word and invited her surrounding neighbors to stop by if they wanted to say goodbye. Martin had been a wonderful novelty to have around and the community was sad to see him leave.

Two weeks earlier Burwell found a pack shovel discarded in the woods and Toby was able to trade it for a rebel boot that almost fit.

One neighbor contributed a dented canteen he'd found and carved a new stopper for. Another found a torn up Yankee shirt and patched it for him.

Boon and Charlotte fashioned a walking staff for him from a heavy hickory tree branch.

The ladies in the community scrounged enough heavy cotton material to sew up a pair of trousers.

A local basket maker fashioned a wide brimmed, palm leaf hat that would help protect him from the sun.

He looked like a picture puzzle where nothing quite matched. But he didn't care, he'd get by.

The evening before he left, Miss Lorraine showed up. She also had some things to give him – including one very unusual gift.

It was a very large, black dog of indeterminable parentage but with amazing skills according to Miss Lorraine. Was this what the locals thought was the bear that stayed back in the tree line when she came calling?

Martin was flabbergasted! A dog?

"His name *Ombrage*. Means *Shadow*. He watch over you. Even if you don't see 'im, he be there. Keep 'im as long as you need 'im – but I want 'im back some day."

She then whispered something in the dog's ear and brought him up to sniff Martin over. Martin bent down and patted him ... and that was it. The bond had been made.

She then reached into her mysterious bag and withdrew a small but colorful necklace made of beads, bones and feathers. She tied it around Martin's neck with a leather cord.

"You meet bad people on your walk, show them this. When you get to where you're going, tie it around neck of Ombrage. He'll come back to me."

She then looked intently at Martin and with her black eyes twinkling, and in a soft voice said, "*Go n-eiri an t-adh leat.*" She gave both his arms a squeeze, turned and retreated into the woods. Ombrage watched her go ... but stayed by Martin's side.

"What she say?" Tanya asked.

"She talked to me in Irish," he said with a look of bewilderment on his face. "She wished me *Good Luck*. I understood what she said ... so I guess I can speak Irish, too. I don't get it. How could she speak Irish? This is all very strange."

32

Banjo survived the operation.

After they took his arm in the field hospital near Mobile they kept him for a week to be sure no infection set in. If it had there was really nothing that could be done anyway. He'd most likely not survive.

But Banjo was one of the lucky ones, most weren't. At the end of the week he was pronounced well enough to travel.

For an additional agonizing week he rode in the back of a wagon and by freight train to a more permanent hospital near St. Louis.

As he slowly regained his strength he tried his best to find out what happened to his friend, Martin.

"Looking for a Martin Shannon," he asked everyone he met. "Eighth Iowa Infantry. Battle of Spanish Fort. Ever hear of him?"

No one had. Indifferent shakes of heads were all he received. The closest he came to any real information was from a damaged old sergeant who overheard him one day.

"Eighth Iowa?" he said. "Had a buddy in that group. Corky O'Connor. Heard they got mustered out quite a while ago. Your pal's probably home by now."

Banjo spent two weeks in the hospital while his strength slowly returned. His lungs cleared up and he was beginning to get used to having one arm. He was fortunate it was his left arm that was taken. He'd already lost part of the hand to frostbite on that arm.

His right arm was intact and that was his best one. He felt very fortunate.

He returned to Dubuque by r i v e r b o a t   i n   e a r l y summer.

Shortly after he arrived, he stopped at the lumber mill and talked to James Brogan, Mary's brother. He asked about Martin and was told he was still missing and presumed dead. He was also told there was a job waiting for him back at the mill when he was ready to come back.

James invited him home for dinner that weekend to meet and talk with Mary. Banjo surely wasn't keen about it, but he knew it was something he had to do.

That night, after dinner, the children were put to bed and the adults retired to the porch where Banjo answered all their questions the best he could.

He told them how good a friend Martin had been to him and how he most likely wouldn't have survived without his help.

He told them all he remembered about that day at Spanish Fort – the last day he'd seen Martin. He stressed he could very well still be alive and stuck in some hospital somewhere like he'd been.

"I found Martin to be very resourceful," he said. "I sure wouldn't give up on him if I was you. If anyone can beat the odds, I'd put my money on Martin every time."

They all realized it was a kind thing for him to say, but no one really believed that would happen.

It was a difficult time for everyone. As might be expected Mary cried most of the evening.

33

Martin left early in the morning.

He shared breakfast with Tanya's family and thanked them all for helping him. He said he'd never forget what they all did for him and if he survived the trip he promised to come back one day and tell them about it in person.

He hoisted a homemade pack on his back, grabbed his walking stick and headed north on a trail they recommended that led through the bayous and swampy landscape. Ombrage was by his side.

Although the city of Mobile was less than fifteen miles away, neither Tanya nor Toby had ever been there. They felt it was too large and they knew no one who lived there that might be able to help him anyway.

Besides, Mobile lay on the western shore of the large bay and he needed to go north.

Initially the path was easy to follow. Only a couple of feet wide it followed the edge of the swampy ground. Tanya's children knew it like the back of their hands and showed him what to look for; brakes in the cane, flattened swamp grasses and openings in the spindly pine thickets. They showed him how to use the stick to check for snakes.

He walked steadily until midday before he took a rest. He'd gone way beyond any area he was familiar with and now needed to pay close attention to what he was doing. He'd seen no sign of other people which didn't surprise him. He was told the area he was heading into held very little human traffic for quite a ways.

Occasionally Ombrage would stop and stare silently into the dismal woods. On a couple of occasions he emitted a deep, low growl and the hair on his back raised; but whatever danger he sensed was short lived.

Martin watched him and took his cue from his behavior.

Several times he'd come across a snake slithering across their path. Ombrage would stand back and bark like crazy to be sure Martin became aware of the danger.

While he rested, Martin ate a couple of pieces of dried fish and one of the hard biscuits Tanya had packed for him. Occasionally he snacked from a bag of nuts and dried berries she also put in for him.

In the bottom of the pack he found a surprise supply of coffee beans she stashed away. He knew how precious they were and planned to use them sparingly. Again he was taken aback at their unselfish generosity.

He only filled his canteen from streams that Ombrage would drink from although he had no idea how the dog knew the water was safe.

Whenever Martin offered him a bite of fish or biscuit, he just turned away. He never did accept anything from him and Martin never did figure out for sure what he ate.

He suspected he did his own hunting and sometimes would hear a yelp or squeal a ways off in the bayou. Some poor creature encountering Ombrage he thought. In any case, he never looked hungry or thirsty.

Twilight came early in bayou country. Heavy layers of Spanish moss that draped down over the cypress and tupelo trees cut down on any sunlight and made it difficult to see the trails.

One thing he was warned about was the danger of getting mixed up and wander around in the dark. He was told that could have fatal results.

Before it got too dark he found a flat piece of ground and made camp. He figured they had gone around ten miles. Not bad for their first day.

The site he chose was away from any boggy grounds and was plentiful with firewood. Sleeping out was second nature to him by now.

Although he still didn't remember any details, he'd been camping out in the open for over two years by this time.

He set out a couple of snares around the edge of the woods. He had enough dried fish and biscuits to last a few days, but soon would have to forage for himself.

When it got dark enough, he found a clearing in the trees and checked the sky to find the North Star – the drinking gourd. He wanted to make sure sure he was still on track.

After eating, he unrolled his palm sleeping pad, covered up with a lightweight blanket and soon fell asleep. Ombrage scanned the area looking for signs of danger. Satisfied there were none, he plopped down beside him, ears erect and alert.

In the morning he found a plump rabbit caught in one of the snares; the other held a possum. He let the possum go. It wasn't that he was adverse to eating possum, but knew the rabbit would be much tastier.

He quickly cleaned it, skinned it and roasted it for breakfast. Along with a biscuit and weak coffee it wasn't much, but he'd get by. He planned to keep the animal skins with him.

He and Ombrage walked for over a week without seeing anyone. Every day he sensed they were making better and better time. It felt good to be walking again and his strong legs responded well.

According to what Miss Lorraine told him, he knew that sooner or later he'd come to a village where he'd use the skins to barter with. If not, he could always do some part-time labor for food.

It was sooner than later.

He knew something was up when one afternoon Ombrage perked up and looked intently ahead.

They soon came across a elderly negro man fishing in a small stream. They saw each other about the same time and were equally startled.

"Afternoon," said Martin as he got closer. "Any luck?"

"Few bream," the man said holding up a stringer with four plump fish, all the while staring at them not quite believing what he was looking at.

"Live nearby?" Martin asked.

"Stockton."

"Stockton?" Martin said. "Far?"

"Ain't."

"Thank you," Martin said and continued on his way, Ombrage not far behind. The old man just sat and stared until they were well out of sight.

"We maybe scared that old man, Ombrage. Think we look strange? 'spect we do. These homemade clothes and mismatched boots do look a little odd if you think about it. And you? You're not exactly a cuddly little 'lap dog'. Well, that's just going to be the way it is for awhile."

Soon Martin heard the unmistakable sounds of civilization; people's voices and children laughing. Someone hammering on some boards. A couple of dogs barking. Ombrage went on full alert. They had arrived at the outskirts of Stockton.

It turned out to be a tiny little settlement but he was excited. It would be his first experience seeing any new people in several months.

The trail widened out a bit and passed by a handful of old wood shacks. One negro lady was outside hanging up washing to dry, her two boys stopped playing and stared as Martin arrived.

"Afternoon," Martin said with a wave.

They silently waved back.

"Place I could get some water?" he asked the lady. "Drank mine all up."

"Pump in the square," she said, looking him over carefully.

"Square?" Martin said looking around. He saw nothing but a handful of broken down shacks and what might have been a church. At least it had a rickety, makeshift steeple.

"Where's the square?"

"Take 'im to the square," she said to the two boys.

They took off like rockets running down a narrow dirt road, waving at Martin to follow.

The square turned out to be patch of ground a couple of blocks ahead; no more than 30 by 50 feet. Apparently someone in Stockton had been to larger towns and decided that every town of any worth was supposed to have a square.

And sure enough, there was an old hand pump right in the middle. Nearby sat several elderly negro men playing checkers on a hand-made board.

A couple of nosy dogs rushed to approach Ombrage but quickly changed their minds and retreated to the safety of one of the buildings.

Everything came to a screeching halt when Martin arrived. The checker players froze, the boys sat on the ground and watched. A few locals started drifting in sensing something was amiss.

Martin filled his canteen, took a long drink and refilled it to the top.

"Mind if a sit and rest a bit?" Martin said to the men. "Been walking all morning."

That seemed to snap the spell.

"Sure," said one man pushing over a chair. "Sit here. Where you heading?"

"Heading north. Going home."

"Where you come from?" another man said.

"Been soldiering – got hurt at Spanish Fort."

No reaction.

" – down by Mobile?" Martin added. "Left there a couple of weeks ago."

"You a Yankee? said the first man. "Don't sound like no Yankee,".

"I'm Irish, Irish Yankee."

"Never heard 'bout them," said the second man. "Where your home?"

"'Can't remember. Lost my memory in the fight. Cannon fire. A few months ago. Lost my hearing, too, but it's mostly come back."

By this time the washer woman and a few of her friends had come in to listen to what the stranger had to say. It was probably the biggest event to come to Stockton since the end of the war.

"You say you going home ... but you can't 'member where home is?" said the washer woman.

"Yes, ma'am," said Martin. "Some nice folks who live near Spanish Fort took care of me. Said I lived somewhere up north.

"'Follow the drinking gourd' is what they told me to do. So that's what I'm doing."

That certainly got their attention. How come this scruffy-looking, strange-talking white man know about the drinking gourd?

"So how will you know when you gets there?" another woman asked incredulously.

"Don't know, ma'am. I hope my memory's back by then ... or someone who knows me sees me."

As they sat there digesting this amazing piece of information one of the older men spotted the necklace.

"What's you got 'round your neck?" he asked.

"This?" said Martin, reaching in and lifting out the necklace for all to see. "A lady ... a Miss Lorraine ... gave this to me."

There was audible gasp when the adults saw the necklace. Several took a step backwards.

"This Miss Lorraine a voodoo lady?" The man asked in a frightened voice.

"I don't know what that is," said Martin. "But she helped heal me. That's her dog over there."

Ombrage was sitting at the side of the square watching the proceedings. He wasn't growling or anything, just sitting quietly and watching.

Everyone turned and saw Ombrage and without another word quickly got to their feet and began to leave.

In less than a minute Martin and Ombrage were left standing there alone.

"Well that was strange," said Martin. "Looks like we're not much welcome here, Ombrage. C'mon. Let's go."

34

The next couple of weeks passed smoothly. Martin and Ombrage were still making good time on their trek north.

They slowly left the critter-infested bayou country behind and were now passing through heavily wooded areas on a variety of old Indian trails and lightly-used trapper paths.

Martin was happy to see fewer and fewer snakes slithering across their path but now had a concern for larger critters.

The few people they infrequently encountered told him the area had a large population of black bears. However once they saw Ombrage they thought he'd have no problem. They were right.

Early one evening they came across a large black bear wandering down the trail toward them, looking like it owned the place.

Ombrage immediately rushed at it with a fearsome barrage of barking and growling and display of sharp teeth. The bear stopped in its tracks and immediately took off into the woods crashing headlong through the underbrush to get away.

"Good dog, Ombrage," said Martin. "You showed that baby who's boss."

The supply of foodstuffs Martin took with him from Tanya's were long gone. For the past several weeks he'd been living off the land.

There was plenty of opportunities to catch fish and he was always able to snare enough small game; rabbits, squirrels, possum and an occasional partridge to fix a fine stew.

That's just what he was doing at dusk one evening when two Confederate soldiers came down the trail, heading south. Like him they were headed for home.

They stopped when they came near his camp and shouted out a greeting.

They looked road-weary and hungry. Martin felt sorry for them and invited them to join him for dinner.

"I have a bit of stew. Should be enough for all of us," Martin said. "Sit down and relax. Where y'all headed?"

"Louisiana," said one. "Name's Homer. This here's Delbert. Thanks for the invite."

Homer was a tall, frail-looking man around thirty years old, heavily bearded, wearing a mishmash of torn clothing and had his left arm in a sling. The arm was wrapped in bandages crusted with dried blood and red dirt.

Delbert was stockier, but much shorter, also bearded and wearing mismatched pants and shirt. He was barefooted and walking with a homemade crutch.

"Which way you headed?" asked Homer.

"North," said Martin. "Been walking several weeks now."

"You a Yankee?"

"I am," said Martin. "Got hurt down south in Alabama. Trying to get home."

"Yeah. We are too," said Delbert. "Got shot up by you damn Yankees up in Tennessee."

"Sorry to hear that," said Martin.

"Yeah, well you'll also be sorry to hear the Yank that busted up my leg is now lying dead in a ditch."

"Delbert," Homer said in a quiet, embarrassed voice. "War's over."

"Maybe for him it is," said Delbert. "Us. We're headed back to a land wasted by them damn Yankees."

"Your friend's right," said Martin, getting slightly annoyed. "War's over. 'Spect I didn't enjoy it any more than you did. You want some stew or not?"

"We sure do," said Homer. "Don't pay attention to Del. His leg's cracked and hurting a bit. That stew

197

smells fine. We've got a little hardtack and coffee we can share."

Martin was planning on saving some of the stew for breakfast but they polished it off as if it were the first decent meal they'd had in a long time.

The hardtack and coffee were a wonderful addition to their meal. Martin surely missed the taste of coffee. The meagre supply Tanya had given him was long gone. He was planning to figure out a way to barter or work for some at the next settlement he came to.

By the time they finished eating it was already dark as pitch in the woods. Martin wasn't comfortable doing so but he told them they were welcome to share his fire for the night. Homer readily accepted for both of them.

They swapped stories awhile but soon got ready to turn in. It was obvious they were dead tired. Homer flopped down where he stood and lasted about 30 seconds before he began snoring.

Martin washed out the stew pot and sat down savoring the coffee by the fire. He took off the boots and put them by his pallet.

Delbert was watching him very carefully – staring at the boots sitting on the ground.

"Like your boots," he said. "Looks like one's Yankee and other's Confederate. That right?"

"Yep. Lost my other down at Spanish Fort. Found this one in the woods."

"Interested in trading 'em?" Delbert said. "Be willing to trade for some hardtack and coffee.'"

"No thanks," said Martin. "Believe I'll keep 'em."

"I lost mine up Tennessee way. Mind if I try 'em on?"

"Don't think so," said Martin. "No sense to it. I don't want to trade. I still have a long ways to go."

After a long pause Delbert said, "Well, how about you just gives 'em to me."

Martin looked up and saw the man had come closer and was now standing by the side of the fire gripping a large Bowie knife. It was pointed right at Martin's heart.

"Are you crazy, man?" Martin said in a voice loud enough to wake up Homer. "What the hell's wrong with you? That's not funny."

Homer woke in a rush, jumped up and shouted, "Delbert! Put that knife down."

"Not 'till this damn Yank gives me those boots," he said as he started to move toward Martin.

It happened in a flash. Like a demon possessed, Ombrage came charging out of the darkness, leaped across the fire and sunk his teeth in Delbert's arm.

He immediately dropped the knife and fell to the ground trying to free himself while howling in fear and pain.

For a few moments, Martin and Homer stood in shock absorbing the scene. Then Martin screamed, "Ombrage - BACK!"

Ombrage immediately released his grip on Delbert's arm and slowly backed away, teeth bared and growling menacingly.

"That your dog?" said Homer while scooting as far away from Ombrage as he could. "Didn't know you had a dog."

"He's mine," said Martin. "Your friend Delbert's lucky he's still alive."

Delbert by this time was sitting up, fearfully looking at Ombrage and inspecting his bleeding arm to see how much damage was done.

"Dog's tore my arm," he said. "It's bleeding bad."

"Could have been your throat," Martin said. "Bandage it up and then you two get the hell outta here. I went and shared my dinner and invited you to stay here in my camp. And this is the thanks I get?"

"Listen, we're sorry, mister," said Homer lifting his hands – palms facing Martin. "Really sorry. I'll make sure it won't happen again."

"You've got about 30 seconds to clear out of here!" Martin said.

"Mister. Don't make us hike outta here in the dark." Homer pleaded. "This here's bear country."

"Should have thought about that earlier," Martin said. "Now go ahead and git!"

"Damn Yankees," Delbert mumbled as he began to reach down for the knife.

"You can just leave that!" Martin said kicking the knife out of his reach. "Just get outta here. And don't even think about trying to sneak back on me. Dog's got your scent now. He'll be waiting for you."

Ombrage knew they were talking about him and he stood woodenly and stared at the two of them.

The hair on his back raised up and he emitted a low, rumbling growl.

They turned away and left hurriedly.

"Good dog. You sit and watch." Martin said as he picked up and admired the Bowie knife. "I wonder who they stole this from. Looks like a Yankee knife. Should come in handy, for sure."

35

Within the next few weeks Martin and Ombrage arrived at a wide river which he later learned was very close to the Alabama state line. Across the river was the town of Florence and a short ways further north was the State of Tennessee. They'd come a long ways. Close to 400 miles he reckoned.

By this time the hard living had taken a toll on his clothes which had been slowly deteriorating and were now not much more than worn out, ripped scraps. He'd tried to keep them as clean as possible, rinsing them in streams along the way; but with only moderate success. Most of the shirt buttons were missing and the pants were ripped off below the knees.

"Ombrage, it's time to take a break and regroup," he said. "If I can find a few day's work, I'll be able to buy some new clothes and stock up on supplies.

"Looking like swamp rats, we're sure to scare the wits out of most people. We've got to spruce up some. What do you think?"

Ombrage just stared at him and whined softly.

"I'll take that as a 'yes'," Martin said.

The trail led down to the river's edge where he found a handful of people waiting for a makeshift ferry to come take them across. Martin looked out in the river and saw the ferry coming, now over half way there.

No one said anything to him, but nodded and stared. He may have looked odd, but probably no odder than the ragtag bunch of hunters, farmers and trappers staring back at him and Ombrage.

The ferry was no more than a flat bottom scow measuring ten by eight feet with rickety looking sides to hold on to. The man running the ferry was hand pulling a rope that spanned the width of the river, less than sixty yards wide at this point. He pulled up to the side of the bank as the people scurried on.

The man looked at Martin and said, "Twenty five cents. Coin only, no script."

"Don't have any money," Martin said. "Would you take some rabbit pelts?"

"Let me see 'em," he said.

Martin unrolled his pack and showed him the pelts.

"Take four pelts," the man said.

"Four pelts!" Martin said with indignation. "Know how much work went into these prime pelts?"

"Three," the man replied. "Or you can swim."

"Done," said Martin as he peeled off three pelts and handed them over.

Immediately the ferry started back across when Martin noticed Ombrage wasn't with them.

"My dog!" Martin exclaimed. "We left the dog. Ombrage!" he shouted.

Ombrage immediately jumped into the river and started paddling across. There were six people in the ferry. One of them noticed Ombrage swimming and said, "Man, look at that mutt go! Looks like it's gonna beat us across."

"Not likely," said a greasy-looking trapper as he lifted up his rifle and took aim at Ombrage.

"You touch that trigger, mister, and I'll cut your hand off," growled Martin who had rushed over brandishing the Bowie knife. "Dog's mine."

"Whoa, there, friend," said the trapper. "I wasn't gonna shoot him. Just scare him a little."

"You heard what I said," said Martin. "Put the gun down."

"Yeah. Sure," said the trapper who sensed Martin wasn't kidding. "I'm no dog killer," he mumbled.

"Not today, you ain't," said Martin.

As it turned out, Ombrage did beat them to the other side and was standing there waiting as the ferry pulled up to the muddy bank.

"Good dog, Ombrage," Martin said.

Ombrage was watching the trapper very closely, but the trapper wisely headed off in the opposite direction.

Florence was the largest town they'd been to yet; maybe a couple hundred people. Martin asked the ferry man where he might be able to find some work for a few days.

"Might try down at Garretson's Mill," he said. "Straight ahead. Can't miss it. Don't mind hard work, he's always looking for some help.

"Heck of a dog you got there, mister. Wanna sell 'im?"

"Not mine to sell," Martin said. "Just loaned to me for awhile."

"Loaned? What's that mean?"

"He's traveling with me until I get where I'm going. Then I'll send him home."

"Where you going?" he asked.

"Not sure. Heading north," Martin said.

"Yeah? Figured that much. Well good luck to you."

Garretson's was a large lumber yard literally buzzing with activity. Martin was directed to a small, one-room office building right in the middle.

Garretson was a large, middle-aged man, solid and rugged looking. A wicked-looking scar ran across his forehead and his nose looked like it had been broken several times. Not a person to mess with.

Martin told him he wanted to work for a few days to earn enough to buy some supplies for his trip north.

"Ever work in a lumber mill before? Can be hard work, but I pay well."

"I'm a hard worker," Martin said, "and a quick learner. Only need to be told once."

Garretson looked him over and made a quick decision. "All right. Go find Johnson in the stripping shed. Tell 'im I said okay. When can you start?"

"Now," Martin said.

Garretson smiled and said, "Off you go then."

Johnson was a huge negro in charge of a crew stripping the bark off large mahogany and oak logs and running them through a monstrous band saw, cutting them into various lengths of building lumber. Most the crew were negroes.

"Got any problem working with coloreds?" he asked. "Don't need no trouble here."

"No trouble. Coloreds saved my life down in Alabama."

"All right then. Stash your pack along the wall and start stacking those boards into piles," he said pointing to a tall stack of freshly sawed lumber. "You just passing through, ain't ya. Which way you heading?"

"North. Been walking for several weeks. Got banged up at Battle of Spanish Fort down near Mobile. Heading home."

"That your dog?" he said, nodding to Ombrage. Can't come in the shed."

"Yeah. It's mine. He won't be no trouble."

"Damn big is what he is," said Johnson. "I 'spect nothing much bothers him."

"Not that I've seen yet," said Martin. "But he minds me."

Martin led Umbrage out by the entrance and told him to stay. The dog dropped in place and stared, taking in the scene. Not a murmur out of him.

Martin worked hard all afternoon, only stopping occasionally for a drink of well water. Like all the other workers he soon stripped to the waist because of the heat. Everyone noticed his scarred up back but didn't say anything. The men mainly stared at his necklace but quickly looked away when Martin looked at them.

Garretson stopped by once to check up on him, seemed satisfied and moved on.

At 6:00, Johnson came over and told him it was time to quit. He looked over at the pile of lumber he been working on, seemed impressed and asked where he was staying for the night.

Martin told him he didn't have a place. Said he'd been camping out at night, and just needed a place to fix a fire and roll out his mat.

Apparently he wasn't the only transient passing through because Johnson told him about a shady clearing nearby that others had used. A creek ran through it.

"How long you figure on staying?" Johnson asked.

"Long enough to buy some new clothes and supplies," Martin said. "A few days anyway. Rest up a bit."

"Work begins at sunup."

"I'll be here," Martin said. "Can I ask you something?"

"What?"

"Noticed all the men staring at me. Don't know why. I know my back's all scarred, is that it."

"It's that thing around your neck," Johnson said, nodding toward Martin's neck. "They saying that's a voodoo necklace. Makes 'em nervous is all."

"Someone else said something 'bout that," said Martin. "Not sure what it means. A colored lady, Miss Lorraine, gave this to me down south. She helped cure me. Said it was good luck. That's her dog over there. Loaned him to me for the trip."

"Listen, mister," said Johnson after a moment's reflection, "I'm a church-going man myself. Don't put much truck in superstition, but I be you, best keep that information to yourself."

The next few days passed uneventfully. The work was hard but Martin was careful to do more than his fair share. He was paid each day; eight cents an hour and was soon able to afford a new set of traveling clothes.

The men, all of them, were used to having him around by this time and seemed to relax a bit in his presence. There was even some light-hearted banter about his Irish accent and Martin taught them a few simple words in Irish which they took great amusement in practicing.

Ombrage kept his distance and the men thought it best to leave it that way.

And then something unexpected happened. He began to remember things.

36

One afternoon Johnson told Martin about a picnic at his church that weekend. Said most of the guys were going and he was welcome to join them.

"Be fun," he said. "A little singing and dancing and lots of good food. The church ladies put it on and all you need do is listen to a few preacher words. Be no drinking ... but some of the boys may sneak a snort or two on the way there," he laughed.

"Sounds nice," Martin said, "What kind of music? I miss hearing music."

"Oh, just simple country tunes," Johnson said. "Mainly strumming and picking, a little harmonica playing. One of the best banjo pickers for miles around will be there. He's a real favorite with the locals ..."

He stopped talking because Martin looked like he was about ready to go into shock.

"What's wrong? You feeling okay?" Johnson asked.

Martin was standing there with his mouth open. His face scrounged up like he was in deep, deep thought. "Banjo," he said. "Banjo ... oh Sweet Jasus – Banjo! Banjo Porter! He was my friend."

Johnson knew Martin couldn't recall much of anything after he'd been hurt in Spanish Fort. He'd heard the story about him losing his hearing *and* his memory.

"You 'membering something?" he said.

"I remember *him*," Martin said. "He was my best friend. We fought together for months and months. We were at Spanish Fort together when I got blown up. I've always wondered what happened to him. When you said 'Banjo' it just came back to me."

Mr. Garretson heard what happened and came to see Martin the next day.

"Johnson told me what happened yesterday. 'Bout you remembering your friend's name. And you wondering about where he is. Is there a chance he could have been killed in the same battle you were in? Sounds like *you* were lucky – maybe he wasn't."

"I don't think so," Martin said. "I checked all the markers before I left and there wasn't any Porter grave that I could find. I'm hoping he got out of it okay."

"I hope he did, too," said Garretson. Hell, maybe he's home by now. You think of that?"

"Yeah," said Martin, "I did ... but he was real close to me when I got blown up. I don't see how he could have gotten out of it in one piece. Odds are he's stuck in a hospital somewheres down here."

"Well, I know there's a bunch of Yankee hospitals up in Tennessee near Franklin," he said. "If you continue going north, you're sure to pass right by. You can ask about your friend there."

Martin left the next week. He was wearing new clothes, including boots, and had a full pack of supplies. He'd stayed longer than planned but he was glad he did. Both he and Ombrage were well rested.

"Thanks for taking me on for awhile," he told Mr. Garretson. "I enjoyed the break."

"Not sure how much of a break it was," Garretson said with a chuckle. "Johnson told me you were a solid worker. You'd be welcome back here any time."

"Thank you, sir. But my first hope is to find my way home."

"Well good luck to you, young man. I hope you do find your way home ... wherever it is."

Ten days latter, Martin and Ombrage were already well into Tennessee. They'd been making solid progress on trails that were well-used and clearly-marked although by this time Martin was as clever as an Indian in spotting even the sparsest of trails.

The bayou country was way behind them now, and they were traveling though heavily-wooded hill country.

There was hardly a day that passed that they didn't encounter either trappers, hunters, carpetbaggers or returning Confederate soldiers.

He no longer feared problems with these strangers. With the ever present Ombrage by his side, Miss Lorraine's necklace around his neck and the carefully-honed Yankee dagger within reach, he almost felt invincible.

He also suspected that word about him and Ombrage had preceded them.

One afternoon he came upon a negro riding a mule laden down with cane.

"How much further to Franklin?" he asked.

"Five ... six miles," the man answered, never taking his eyes off Ombrage."

"Looking for a friend might be in an army hospital. Know of any hospitals there?"

"Know there's plenty of hospitals. Won't be hard to find one."

The Battle of Franklin, Tennessee, was fought at the end of 1864 just four months before the Battle of Spanish Fort. It was a horrendous fight with over 10,000 killed, mainly Confederates, during a terrible five-hour period. The result of this bloodbath saw the establishment of over 40 field hospitals in the area.

At this point, Martin had begun to accept the improbable task of trying to track down Banjo. As far as he knew, Banjo may not have even gotten this far. All he could do was try ... try and hope for the best.

It took a while before he found the building where records were kept. As it turned out, it was all a great waste of time.

When he finally did locate someone alert enough to answer any questions, Martin was unable to tell him what army unit they fought with. He simply couldn't remember and he explained how he lost his memory, just recently remembering the name of his friend.

"So what *can* you tell me?" the clerk asked. "Where were you fighting when you got hurt?"

"Spanish Fort," Martin quickly said. "Down in Alabama."

"Yeah, I know where it is. We did have some men pass through here from Spanish Fort. I seem to recall they were mainly from Illinois. You're Irish aren't you?"

"I am indeed," Martin said.

"And you don't know where your home is?"

"Can't remember."

"Well, if I was you. I'd head towards Chicago, lots of Irish troops came from there."

"How far's Chicago?" Martin asked.

"A long ways. 'Bout 500 miles I believe," the clerk said. "But I'll tell you something that might be of some help to you. I heard there's new track laid now from Owensboro clear to Chicago. Owensboro's in northern Kentucky ... maybe 150 miles from here. You make it that far?"

"'Spect I can," Martin said with a grin. "Walked over 500 miles just to get here. Another 150 won't bother me none."

Two weeks later Martin and Ombrage arrived at Owensboro. The countryside they'd passed through to get there still looked war weary but Martin couldn't help but notice people were digging their way out of the destruction, little by little.

The clerk in Franklin was right. The railroad lines torn up during the war were being repaired as quickly as possible. Teams of roustabouts, mainly negroes, were laying down ties and pounding in the spikes as soon as they were unloaded by mule-driven carts.

Martin asked around and found a foreman in charge of one of the crews.

"Understand the line's open to Chicago," he said.

"Tis," said a burly-looking chap speaking in a lovely Irish accent, all the while giving Martin and Ombrage the once over. "No passenger cars running yet if that's what you're getting at."

"I'll ride in anything," Martin said. "Been walking over 600 miles just to get this far. Trying to get home. Got wounded down at Spanish Fort near Mobile – got left behind."

"You a County Kerry man aren't you?" the foreman asked with a twinkle in his eye.

"For sure, I am," Martin replied in a startled voice. "Raised in Scartaglen." *(Scartaglen! Where did that come from? I'm from Scartaglen, County Kerry?)*

"Thought so," said the man holding out his hand. "Got a good ear for accents, I do. Name's Michael Foley – a Clare man meself."

"Martin Shannon," said Martin gripping the hand. "Pleased to meet you, Mr. Foley."

"So it's Chicago you want to go? That's where you joined up, is it?"

"To be honest, Mr. Foley," Martin said. "I'm not sure. I got banged up in battle and lost my hearing *and* my memory. Hearing's come back, but I'm still having trouble remembering most things. But Chicago sounds familiar."

"Oh, I hope you're right," said Foley. "It's a grand city. I'm from there meself. I'm heading up one of several teams down here getting this track laid. Working our way down to Nashville before I go back. Hard job, but the pay's grand."

"Do you think I could get a ride to Chicago?"

"Well, I'll tell you what," Foley said after a moment's consideration. "There's a supply train coming in sometime tonight. As soon as it's unloaded, it's heading right back, be sometime early in the morning. I can fix it for you to ride on one of the flatbeds. Be a rough ride though. Interested?"

"That's fine with me," Martin said. "I suspect I've ridden on many flatbeds when soldiering,"

"Okay then. You can camp in the rail yard tonight if you want. Be ready to go when you hear the whistle. But you won't be able to take your dog with you."

"That's all right. I'm going to send him back to Alabama anyway. He was just loaned to me."

"Loaned? The dog can find his way back alone?" Foley asked. "Clear to Alabama?"

"This dog can." Martin said.

Martin had a restless night's sleep. The sound of the roustabouts unloading the train went on all night long. It was about dawn before things started to quiet down and Martin knew it wouldn't be long before they'd get ready to leave.

He called Ombrage over to him.

"You've been a good friend, Ombrage," he said scratching the dog's ears. "I would never have gotten this far without you. I'm surely going to miss you."

He untied the necklace Miss Lorraine had given to him and, as instructed, tied it around Ombrage's neck.

"It's time for you to go back home, boy. I'll be fine from here on. Be careful, you hear? Now go!"

Ombrage stood in place seemingly unsure what was going on. He stared into Martin's eyes and whined softly.

"Go home, Ombrage," he said waving his hand in a southernly direction. "Go home, boy. I'll come back and see you one day. I promise. You go on now."

Ombrage finally started to trot away, went around 100 yards, paused and looked back to see Martin still waving him away. Then he turned south and ran off.

37

CHICAGO

Fall 1865

Martin ate a quick breakfast, rolled up his pack and headed toward the train. He no sooner got there when the whistle sounded.

Michael Foley was waiting for him and introduced him to the engineer who had already been told he had his permission to ride on one of the flatbeds.

"Good luck, son," he said. "You should get to Chicago sometime late tonight. Hope you find what you're looking for."

"Thanks, Mr. Foley. I appreciate your help ... and I hope I do, too."

The train stopped at Terre Haute, Indiana, early afternoon. They needed to pick up coal and water. The engineer walked back to the flatbed and told Martin they were taking an hour's break.

"How you doing back here?" he said. "Ride a little rough?"

"Not too bad," Martin replied. "I 'spect I've had worse. Is there any place nearby to get something to eat?"

"Little cafe right in the station. Sandwiches and coffee's all."

"That'll do. Need to get up and stretch anyway," Martin said.

"Listen, young fella, looks like we're coming into some weather. Why don't you grab your stuff and join me in the engine. Plenty of room and Foley wouldn't care."

"You sure?"

"Yeah, c'mon. I'd enjoy the company."

Gunter Weiss was a fifty-three-year-old immigrant from Stuttgart, Germany. He'd been driving trains for over twenty years, the last ten of which have been out of Chicago. He and his wife, Gretchen, had a 12-year-old daughter, Anna, and a 15-year-old son, Kurt, living at home. Their oldest son, Eric, had been killed during the Battle of Chattanooga.

Weiss was right about the weather. They'd no sooner pulled out of Terre Haute before the clouds opened up. Martin would have been soaked and miserable the rest of the trip if he'd still been back on the flatbed.

They spent the rest of the afternoon and evening talking about the war and how it's affected everyone in the country.

He told Martin how they lost their eldest son almost two years prior and how difficult that has been on him and his wife.

"Foley told me you were hurt down in Alabama," he said. "Having trouble with your hearing and memory. That right?"

"Yeah," said Martin. "Hearing came back in a few weeks. Memory's taking longer. But I think it's starting. I know my name, of course, and now remember where I was born in Ireland. I even remember the name of one my friends that was with me when we got blown up ... but I can't remember what outfit we were assigned to and that has been the real problem getting any information.

"A hospital clerk down in Tennessee told me there were some Irish guys that passed through his area who had fought at Spanish Fort. Said they were from Chicago and said the odds were that's where I'm from, too. Hoping I find out more when I get there."

"Do you have a place to stay in Chicago?" he asked. "It's a pretty big city you know."

"No I don't," Martin said. "Not even sure where to start looking."

"Why don't you come stay with us," Weiss said. "My wife and I would be happy to have you. At least for a few days, until I have to take off again."

"Really?" Martin said. "Sure I won't be too much trouble?"

"Not at all," Weiss said. "We have extra space now that Eric's gone. And after we get to town I can ask around and find some places where you can make inquiries about your friend. Do you have any money?"

"Yeah, I have a little," Martin said. "Saved it from a job I had along the way. I can always earn some more when I need it."

The train pulled into the Chicago station around 8:30 that evening. Martin recognized it instantly.

"I've been here before," he excitedly told Weiss. "I remember this station. We came in from New York!"

"Really?" Weiss said. "Who's we?"

That stopped Martin again. He strained at trying to recall ....

"Can't remember for sure," he said. "Two others I think ... and maybe women ..."

"Hey, that's great," said Weiss. "You *are* starting to remember more. I bet when you see some places you've been to, more and more memories will come back to you."

"I sure hope so," said Martin. "At least that's what I'm planning for."

Martin met Mrs. Weiss and their children later that evening. They lived in the north side of Chicago in the German section of town.

Their spotless apartment was large with a parlor, three bedrooms, a small kitchen, a back porch and fenced in yard. The kitchen had a wash basin for cleaning up and meal preparation. They shared an outside toilet with the apartment above them.

There was also a bathhouse at the end of the block they all used once a week.

Mrs. Weiss and the kids had already eaten but she prepared a light meal for them while Martin told the family a little about himself and his adventures after leaving Alabama that Spring.

Mr. Weiss could hardly believe he's walked as far as he had ... over 600 miles?

Mrs. Weiss was fascinated to hear about his memory loss. She'd heard about such things but had never actually met anyone that was affected.

The children, especially Karl, the son, wanted to know more about Ombrage.

"You left him in Tennessee?" he asked.

"I had to," Martin said. "Couldn't take him on the train."

"But who'll take care of him," asked Anna. "He'll got lost and die."

"Not Ombrage," Martin said. "I bet he's halfway home by now."

"But how will he find his way ..."

"All right, children," Mrs. Weiss interrupted. "That's enough questions for tonight. "I'm sure

Martin is quite tired and would like to rest. Besides you both have school tomorrow.

"Kurt, you take Martin back to your room and show him Eric's bed. You let him sleep now. No more questions, hear?"

"Yes, mama."

"Martin," said Mr. Weiss. "We'll go back to the station tomorrow and see if we can find out anything about your friend. "I've got some reports to fill out at the office and check on my next assignment."

Martin followed Kurt down the dark hall, leaving the parents talking together quietly in German.

Mrs. Weiss was right. He was almost dead on his feet. He quickly undressed and slipped in between the crisp clean sheets. He'd forgotten how wonderful a real bed felt. He couldn't remember how long it had been since he'd last slept in one.

His last thoughts before he drifted off into a deep, silent slumber were of the old country ... of a salty breeze blowing in from the Irish Sea and over the green cliffs of County Kerry. Of his ma's sweet voice singing lovely old Irish ballads to him and Colleen by the fire. The pungent tobacco smell from his da's pipe.

It all seemed so long ago and far away ...

38

Martin woke as his shoulder was being being lightly shaken by Mr. Weiss. He felt groggy and for a moment couldn't remember where he was.

"Wake up, Martin," he said. "It's almost noon, son. You've been asleep 15 hours! Get dressed and come and eat something before we head to the station."

Kurt and Anna were big hits at school that day, telling all their friends about the mysterious Irish stranger who had come to stay with them.

None of Anna's friends could quite get over the story about sending his dog home alone. Several hundred miles. They all feared for the poor dog's safety.

Kurt friends were more interested in hearing about the scars he'd seen on Martin's back.

"I saw him take off his shirt last night," he said to his wide-eyed companions during lunch period. "His whole back was crisscrossed with scars from shrapnel and burns. And he's got a streak of white hair on the back of his head and part of his ear is missing. And he limps a little."

"Gosh," said Peter Hershel. "He sounds like he's been in a lot of battles. It's amazing he's still alive."

"And that's not all," Kurt said. "He lost his memory. He can't even remember where his home is."

"What?" said another friend. "He can't remember where he was born?"

"Well, he's Irish," said Kurt. "He was born in Ireland ... but he can't remember where he lives *now*. He did tell my father that he's pretty sure he's been to Chicago before, so maybe he lives around here somewhere."

"Wow!" exclaimed Peter. "What's he going to do now?"

He and my father are going to the station today and ask around ... maybe he can remember some more or see someone he knows."

Martin and Mr. Weiss spent most of the afternoon near the depot without any luck. They talked to dozens of war veterans milling around the station but none were able to help.

Eventually one of men directed them to a downtown office where returning veterans reported to apply for wages never paid. Others went there to apply for medical aid.

Although the war had been over for several months there always seemed to be a crowd of veterans and family members lined up waiting to talk to someone.

Martin got in line while Mr. Weiss returned to the station to do his reporting and pick up his next assignment.

"I'll meet you back at the station at 5:00," he said. "Good luck."

It was almost 4:00 p.m. before Martin's name was called. He raised his arm and was pointed to a haggard-looking clerk who looked like he was dead tired after being on his feet all day. He was standing behind a waist-high counter covered with dozens of heavily-used binders.

"I'm looking for any records you might have for a Martin Shannon or Banjo Porter," Martin asked. "Both were injured at the Battle of Spanish Fort, Alabama. Back in March, I believe."

"Yeah? What unit were they in?" asked the bored clerk. "Lots of units were in that fight. Several from this area."

"I don't know the unit," said Martin. "I was hoping you could tell me."

"All our records are listed by unit," replied the clerk. "Nothing is listed by name. Be too many. These guys alive or killed?"

"I don't know about Porter. Shannon's alive. That's me."

"What the hell!" said the clerk in a disgusted manner. "You trying to be funny? Look around you. Can't you see how busy we are. What unit were you in? I asked you that once!"

"I'm sorry. Not trying to be funny. I can't remember much of anything. I lost my memory after the battle."

That stopped the clerk cold. He stared at Martin for a moment. He said, "Look, I'm sorry. You should have said something earlier. You can't remember your unit?"

"No, I can't. I can't even remember where I enlisted. I was hoping you could tell me. I'm trying to find my way back home."

"Wish I could help you," said the clerk already looking past Martin at the crowd behind him. "Come back if you can remember anything more. We really can't help unless we know the unit you were with. Sorry."

Martin and Mr. Weiss headed back to his apartment around 6:00. Martin filled him in on what happened and told him it didn't look very promising.

"Now don't despair Martin," Mr. Weiss said. "I have a new lead. Someone suggested it might be worth a visit to the Hibernian Hall over in the Irish neighborhood. They may be able to help you.

"I don't have to leave town for a couple more days and you're more than welcome to stay with us until then. We'll go there tomorrow."

The Ancient Order of Hibernians had a large meeting hall used for dances, political meetings, wedding parties, sports events and a general catch-all for all neighborhood gatherings of anything to do with Irish interests.

When Martin and Mr. Weiss arrived there was a large group of parents with their children practicing for a dance recital to be held that weekend.

Although Martin was thrilled to hear so many Irish voices being spoken at one place, there was no one there he recognized – and neither was there anyone there who recognized him.

And all the name 'Banjo Porter' gathered were giggles at such a ridiculous name.

"Have you stopped by any of our pubs?" said one fellow just as they were turning to leave. "If anyone knows anything around here that's where I'd go. And even if you don't learn anything, drinking the lovely Guinness would definitely make it worth the trouble."

"Hey, that's a great idea," said Mr. Weiss. "Can you suggest some places? We're not from around here."

"Yeah, I can tell," the man said with a grin. "Well ... for what you're wanting, I'd try Emmet's, for sure ... then The Brazen Head ... and maybe Murphy's. They're all within just a few blocks from here.

"Ask anyone and they'll show you the way ... but tell you what," he said after a moment's reflection. "Soon as I finish up here I'll take you to Emmet's meself. All this talking's made me terrible thirsty."

39

The three of them set off for Emmet's which was, indeed, just a couple of blocks from the hall. They entered a large room filled with locals enjoying a pint with their friends.

"Well, look who the cat just drug in," said the publican standing behind a long walnut bar washing glasses. "Hugh Conner, as I live and breathe. Here to buy the house a round, I suspect."

"Wrong you are, Mr. Cassidy," said Hugh. "But I will stand these two gents to a pint if you'd be so kind ... and I'd like to pose a question to all here if you're sober enough to understand."

That received an equal share of 'boos' and laughs.

With pints in hand, he turned to the room and said, "Gentlemen – I've got a young Kerryman here – Martin Shannon – just home fresh from the war. Seems he's having a wee bit of a memory problem. He'e trying to return home ... but it seems he can't remember where his home is. He wants to know if anyone here recognizes him."

That got everyone's attention and they all stared at Martin shaking their heads one by one.

After a moment Martin asked, "Does anyone here know a man called Banjo Porter?"

Again he was met by silent stares and shaking heads.

"I'm sorry lads," said their friend, Hugh. "I was hoping for better luck. Let's finish up here and I'll walk you to The Brazen Head. It's conveniently on my way home, it is.

After a repeat performance at The Brazen Head Hugh give them directions to Murphy's, bid them good luck and left for his own home.

"Maybe this wasn't such a grand idea after all," Martin said. "Looks like we're just wasting our time."

"Well, let's try Murphy's as long as we're this close," said Mr. Weiss. "At least we know we've taken a good shot at it."

It was early evening by this time and the streets were filling up with kids out playing tag and stick ball. Dogs were running wild, chasing each other with wild abandon. Ladies were chatting together on front porches. The lamp lighter was half way down the street.

They stopped to ask for directions a couple of times and finally turned a corner and there it was – Murphy's Pub – already starting to fill up with thirsty workers on their way home from a hard day on the job.

Martin stopped in his tracks and froze.

"What's wrong?" said Mr. Weiss.

"I've been here before," said Martin.

"You have?" said Mr. Weiss excited. When?"

"Can't remember that." Martin said. "But I'm certain I've been here."

"Alone?"

"Don't think so," Martin said. "It seems like an awful long time ago."

"Well, let's go in and see what we can find out."

Murphy's Pub was crowded – and loud. The two of them drew a few glances but most of the crowd's interest was in the pint glasses of Guinness on the tables in front of them.

Mr. Weiss and Martin worked their way up to the bar and ordered a pair of pints and looked around.

"See anyone you recognize?" asked Mr. Weiss.

"No. Not yet," said Martin looking from face to face. "But I've been in here before. I'm almost sure of it."

Mr. Weiss waved over the publican who just happened to be the owner, Mr. Murphy.

"Two more?" Murphy said.

"No. Not just yet. But I'm wondering if you could help us."

"Well now, what be ye needing?"

"My young Irish friend here is looking for a little help. He's just arrived back from the war. Got hurt pretty bad down in Alabama. He's having trouble remembering things but seems certain he's been in here before."

"Yeah?" said Murphy glancing with curiosity at Martin. "Doesn't look familiar – want I should ask the others?"

"If you wouldn't mind, please," said Mr. Weiss.

"All right, you men," Murphy shouted to the open room, "Quiet down a minute."

No one paid any attention to him.

"QUIET!" he screamed, pounding on the bar with his ham size fists.

That got their attention.

"This Irish gent here," he said, nodding to Martin, "would like to ask you all something. So be polite for a change and listen to what he's got to say."

Martin felt a little foolish but took a deep breath and jumped right in.

"My name's Martin Shannon. I just arrived in Chicago after a long trip, mostly on foot, from Alabama where I was banged up in the Battle of Spanish Fort."

That got their attention.

"I was hurt when a shell went off right in the middle of a bunch of us," Martin continued. "Several of my friends were killed or injured and I lost my hearing and my memory during the explosion. I eventually got my hearing back – but I'm still having trouble remembering things."

At this point you could hear a pin drop.

"I was told quite a few fellows in that battle were from Illinois, and most likely Chicago. I do know I've been in this pub before. It was a long time ago but I'm trying to remember. If I could only find someone who might recognize me and help me remember my past. I'm trying to find my way back home."

The men in the pub listened to what he had to say, shaking their heads and talking among themselves in amazement at the strange story.

"I don't recognize you at all young man," said one man standing close by at the bar. "But you're a brave young Irishman, for sure, and I'll be honored to stand you to a pint."

"I as well," shouted another man.

Soon several others stood and made the same generous offer. Things were livening up.

"So, tell us where you're from in Ireland," shouted one slightly tipsy man. "Sounds like a Cork tongue to me."

"You're daft, man," said another. "He's a Dublin man, through and through."

"Tis not," shouted another. "He's from Clare for sure – and I'd say from Ennis if I had to put a fine point to it."

That opened up a deluge of conflicting opinions until the pushing and shoving started. It all came within a hair's breath of turning into a down and out brawl until Murphy pounded on the bar again and threatened to throw them all out if they didn't settle down.

That would have been an grave injustice – being tossed out with their pints left unfinished – so things quieted down in a hurry.

Just as things got back to normal, an old man who had been sitting, half asleep, back in the corner stood up and said, "I remember the man. He's from Kerry, he is."

Another man laughed and said, "Brian Kavanagh, you can't remember *anything*! Why you forget to button up your trousers half the time."

That brought another rush of laughter.

"Hey! He's right," shouted Martin. "I *am* from County Kerry."

"Lucky guess, Kavanagh," a man said. "Just a lucky guess."

"Is that right?" said Kavanagh, now on a roll. "He's not only from County Kerry – the man's from Scartaglen. And you can put that in your pipe and smoke it!"

"Wait – he's right again," shouted Martin in shock. "Scartaglen, that indeed is where I'm from."

All eyes switched back and forth from Kavanagh to Martin during this strange exchange. It was obvious the crowd was transfixed.

"Good Lord!" said Murphy in a loud voice causing everyone to turn from Martin to look at him. "I remember now! I've met this young man before.

Michael Brogan brought him here one night, him fresh off the boat. Michael and Michael Jr. But – that's been – Good Lord – years ago."

"Brogan!" said Martin in a excited voice. "Yes! I'm remembering it now. Michael and Kate Brogan. Of course, he met us at the train station."

"Met who?" jumped in Mr. Weiss sensing a major breakthrough. "Who were you with on the train?"

" ... I can't remember that," struggled Martin with his eyes closed. "I can't remember ... God, my head hurts."

"Martin, come sit down here," said Mr. Weiss leading him over to a table where several men jumped up to make room for him. "Mr. Murphy, could I trouble you for a glass of water for Martin here?"

Murphy rushed over with a glass of water and said to one of the men standing by, "Byrne, run over to the Brogans. Tell him we've got a Martin Shannon here. Tell 'em to come ... and hurry."

Paddy Byrne took off like a shot – out the door of Murphy's Pub and ran like a banshee the block and a half to the Brogan house.

Kate Brogan and a few neighbor ladies were sitting on the porch visiting. The boys were out playing somewhere. Lily and a couple of her girlfriends were just coming back from a stroll around the park when Paddy Byrne, out of breath, came rushing up to the house.

"Is Michael at home, Mrs. Brogan?" he panted.

"No. He worked late tonight, Paddy. He and Junior are on their way home now. Why? What happened?"

"There's a man down at Murphy's who says he knows you and Michael."

"Sure we know a lot of people, we do. Who is he and what does he want?"

"Not sure what he wants. Says his name's Martin Shannon."

Word quickly spread around the neighborhood about a strange visitor that was in Murphy's Pub. Something about a lost Irish Civil War soldier?

With the unexpected excitement, Murphy was doing a landslide business selling Guinness when suddenly the front door flew open and in rushed the Brogan clan led by Kate Brogan herself.

The men all jumped to their feet and backed away, partly in shock to see a woman enter the time-honored male sanctity of pub grounds, and partly to prepare for the ensuing drama that was sure to follow.

Martin stood and faced the Brogans as they slowly approached him with mouths wide open.

He stared at them smiling sadly as the shackles on his memory slowly began to fall away.

It was all coming back to him now in a rush and he could barely stand it. He finally focused on one very special red haired individual.

He bent down at the waist and said, "Hello Lily."

There was a moment's pause before Lily screamed, "Martin! You're alive!" and rushed into his open arms.

40

The packet boat from Clinton to Dubuque ran every day except Sunday. It left Davenport early in the morning, arrived at Clinton at noon and left shortly thereafter arriving in Dubuque around 6:00 in the evening.

Martin could have waited in Chicago and taken the freight train direct to Dubuque but that service had been reduced to running only twice a month. He surely didn't want to wait that long before he saw Mary again.

The Brogans had talked about wiring her from Chicago but Martin said he didn't want to do that, either. He wanted to be standing in front of her himself when they again met. Face to face.

Traveling by boat on the Mississippi was always a treat, but especially so at this time of year. The Fall leaves covered the hillsides with a splurge of color; a gorgeous mix of burnt orange, deep reds and rich golds.

Martin stood out on deck, breathing in the crisp, fresh air and watched bald eagles soar overhead, searching the water's surface for the hint of a fish.

How long had it been since he'd been heading the opposite direction going south to war? It seemed forever. He recalled how anxious he and his friends were to begin what they all believed would be a six-month enlistment; so full of youthful excitement and hope.

"Three years," he said to himself. "Good Lord, I've been gone almost three years. What am I going to say to her? Will she even recognize me?"

The boat pulled into Dubuque's ice harbor right on time. It was still light out when Martin grabbed his bag, jumped off the boat and headed up the hill towards town. He needed to hurry. It would be dark soon.

It had been over a year since he last heard from Mary. She had written that she was still living with her brother and sister-in-law up on the bluff. Their two children she was taking care of had now become three and he wondered if any more had arrived since.

As he got closer he noticed there were several new houses scattered around their neighborhood that weren't there when he left.

James' house was now surrounded by a large fenced in yard, with a generous section devoted to a vegetable garden.

He didn't remember the trees being that large.

He stopped from afar to slowly take in the scene. He saw Mary in the middle of the garden, filling her apron with tomatoes, perhaps the last of the season. It took all his will power not to scream out to her.

A small girl was helping her pick. There were other kids running around the yard playing tag, laughing and hollering and having a great time.

Her bother, James was sitting out on the porch smoking his pipe and talking to one of the older children who was reading a book. His wife, Maureen was standing in the doorway drying dishes.

Martin paused. A heavy feeling of peace washed over him as he soaked in the loveliness of it all. He opened the gate and stepped into the yard. After a few tentative steps toward the house he stopped.

The children saw him first and quieted down immediately – staring at this strange looking man – someone they had never seen before.

James sensed the change in noise and turned himself and looked at Martin in silence as his brain slowly figured out what was happening – at whom he was seeing.

Maureen also saw him and gave out a soft gasp. She let the dish she was drying fall and shatter on the floor and clutched the towel to her breast.

Without moving James calmly said to the boy sitting near him, "Peter, go fetch your Aunt Mary. Tell her someone's come to see her."

Mary was already on her way back to the house when Peter intercepted her and told her what his father had said.

She stopped and looked at the house. Everyone was staring out into the yard. She turned to see what they were looking at and froze ... dropped the hem of her apron, filled with tomatoes ... letting them roll down the incline.

Martin looked at her and smiled. Then he slowly took off his pack, opened it up and took out a tattered, soiled, faded blue scarf. He held it up for her to see.

"I promised I'd return your scarf, Mary, " he said in a soft voice. "I always keep my promises."

EPILOGUE

Martin and Mary were married at St. Bridget Catholic Church the second Saturday in May.

Mary looked radiant and Martin looked ... well, extremely happy.

Michael and Kate Brogan were there. They brought the flower girl with them from Chicago. Lily never stopped grinning during the entire service.

Banjo Porter was Martin's groomsman and one of Mary's best friends from St. Bridget's was bridesmaid.

The church was packed, with a good share of people coming from Kennedy's Lumber Mill where both Martin and Banjo were working again as they were before the war.

That September Martin returned to Alabama. The war had been over long enough that it was now possible to travel by train from Chicago clear to Mobile on newly-laid track.

Mary traveled with him as far as Chicago and stayed with Uncle Michael and Aunt Kate while Martin picked up some special supplies to take along with him. Mary really didn't like the idea of him leaving again, but she understood the reason why.

Before he left he took her over to meet the Weiss family who had been so kind to him and without whose help he may never have found his way back. As a souvenir, he gave Mr. Weiss the Bowie knife he took from the Confederate soldier.

It was a grueling day and a half ride to Mobile. Martin got off the train around noon. It was less than 15 miles to Fort Blakeley ... or what was left of it and a few more to the settlement.

He caught a packet boat across the bay and started walking. If he was able to walk over 600 miles home, he should be able to handle this short distance.

It wasn't long before he came across some of the trails he had hiked with Tanya and Toby's children. Deep in the bayous now, he felt right at home.

Somehow Miss Lorraine knew he was coming and went to alert the people in the settlement.

"Martin's coming," she said when she found Tanya working in her garden.

"What?" said Tanya. "Who's coming?"

"That soldier boy, Martin," said Miss Lorraine. "Coming to visit. Be here mid-afternoon. Sent Ombrage to fetch him."

"Martin!" said Tanya. "Martin's coming?"

"What I said," replied Miss Lorraine.

And sure enough, later in the afternoon Martin, accompanied by his old friend, Ombrage, came walking up to Tanya and Toby's shack. It was quite a shock for everyone.

That evening all the folks living in the area gathered for an impromptu potluck. Everyone wanted to see Martin and hear what he had to say.

It was the biggest event to happen in the area since the battle itself.

Martin spent hours that evening telling everyone about his trip north. About the snakes, the bears and other critters he came across. About both the good and bad folks he had run into along the way and how Ombrage had saved him from harm on many occasions. He told them how far he walked and how long it took him, neither of which they could hardly believe.

He told them he had all his memory back now and was able to find his way home. He lived in a State called Iowa over 950 miles north from there.

They had no idea of how far 950 miles was. A powerful long ways, is all they knew.

He told them he was now married and working in a lumber mill but took time off to come down and thank everyone personally for being such good friends to him and saving his life.

It was a story that would be repeated to children and grandchildren for generations to come.

The next two days were spent going over the presents he had purchased for the children. Books that would teach them how to read and write. It was probably the best present he could have brought.

Tanya and Toby had never seen a book before and were very grateful. They knew their children were intelligent and now realized if they could learn to read and write, it would provide a better opportunity to improve their lives, something neither of them had ever had the chance to do.

After a few days it was time to go back.

The morning he left they all walked back to the Spanish Fort battle site. Nothing much had changed. Except for a small fenced off burial area, the rest of the grounds were quickly becoming overgrown.

Martin went to see the graves which someone had been taking care of. The area was freshly weeded and had newly-planted flowers around the edge.

There were 12 wooden crosses now with names of each soldier and the outfit he had been attached to etched on the surface. Both Yankee and Confederate burials were mixed together.

A much larger number of crosses read, "Unknown."

Martin saw names of three men who had been with the Eighth Iowa Infantry. He recognized one name as being from Dubuque, the others he wasn't sure about. He wrote them all down.

When he returned home, he'd try to find the families who he suspected had no idea whatever happened to their loved ones.

Then, for the last time, he said his goodbyes to Tanya's family and to Miss Lorraine.

Ombrage sensing he was seeing his friend for the last time whined softly as Martin knelt down and scratched his ears.

"Goodbye, loyal friend," he whispered. "You keep an eye on Miss Lorraine, hear?"

Then he stood up and smiled at all these good people, turned and headed back to Mobile to catch a train.

It was time to go back home for good.

-o-

ABOUT THE AUTHOR

Robert Buckley was born and raised in New York. A graduate of Iowa State University he spent his career in the advertising agency business.

The Saga of Martin Shannon, as well as his five earlier works - *The Slave Tag, Ophelia's Brooch, Two Miles An Hour, The Denarius* and *I'm Lost Again* are all available in eBook as well as printed format on Amazon.com.

Made in the USA
San Bernardino, CA
30 November 2018